There was no possible future between a waitress at the Coach House Diner and a doctor at the Armstrong Institute, Jennifer thought sadly.

Their lives were too different, the disparity in their background and income too great. They wouldn't see each other anymore, outside the diner.

Jennifer knew it was for the best, but somehow the thought of going back to pouring Chance his morning coffee while knowing she'd never be more than a onetime date made her heart ache and tears well.

It's no good yearning for the moon, she told herself stoutly, wiping dampness from her cheeks. *I knew when I agreed to go out with him that it was a onetime thing. No future dates, no building dreams of a relationship.*

She switched off the television and the living-room lamps, then entered her bedroom, where the bedside lamp threw a pool of light over her solitary bed.

It's time for Cinderella to go back to her real life.

D0048715

Dear Reader,

I was intrigued when my editor asked me to be a part of THE BABY CHASE series. First, because fertility clinics can be beacons of hope for couples with fertility issues. And second, because I was charmed by the prospect of writing about a hero who loves women and balances a playboy personality with a passionate commitment to his patients. And third, because I've never been able to resist a romance novel about a rake falling in love at last, especially when the woman who owns his heart is an independent, wary career woman and single mother of an adorable little girl.

I had so much fun watching Dr. Chance Demetrios meet his fate in beautiful Jennifer Labeaux. And to add icing on this particular cake, Chance finds himself feeling ferociously parental and protective toward Annie, Jennifer's adorable little girl. How can you not love a guy who is charmed and enchanted by a red-haired, sweetly precocious child? And how can you not cheer for Jennifer, a woman who's strong enough and wise enough to choose a mate like Chance?

I hope you enjoy reading *Cinderella and the Playboy*— I thoroughly loved writing Jennifer and Chance's story.

Warmly,

Lois Faye Dyer

CINDERELLA AND THE PLAYBOY

LOIS FAYE DYER

Silhouette

SPECIAL EDITION®

Published by Silhouette Books

America's Publisher of Contemporary Romance

If you purchased this book without a cover you should be aware that this book is stolen property. It was reported as "unsold and destroyed" to the publisher, and neither the author nor the publisher has received any payment for this "stripped book."

Special thanks and acknowledgment to Lois Faye Dyer for her contribution to THE BABY CHASE miniseries.

 SILHOUETTE BOOKS

Recycling programs for this product may not exist in your area.

ISBN-13: 978-0-373-65518-2

CINDERELLA AND THE PLAYBOY

Copyright © 2010 by Harlequin Books S.A.

All rights reserved. Except for use in any review, the reproduction or utilization of this work in whole or in part in any form by any electronic, mechanical or other means, now known or hereafter invented, including xerography, photocopying and recording, or in any information storage or retrieval system, is forbidden without the written permission of the editorial office, Silhouette Books, 233 Broadway, New York, NY 10279 U.S.A.

This is a work of fiction. Names, characters, places and incidents are either the product of the author's imagination or are used fictitiously, and any resemblance to actual persons, living or dead, business establishments, events or locales is entirely coincidental.

This edition published by arrangement with Harlequin Books S.A.

For questions and comments about the quality of this book please contact us at Customer_eCare@Harlequin.ca.

® and TM are trademarks of Harlequin Books S.A., used under license. Trademarks indicated with ® are registered in the United States Patent and Trademark Office, the Canadian Trade Marks Office and in other countries.

Visit Silhouette Books at www.eHarlequin.com

Printed in U.S.A.

Books by Lois Faye Dyer

Silhouette Special Edition

Lonesome Cowboy #1038
He's Got His Daddy's Eyes #1129
The Cowboy Takes a Wife #1198
The Only Cowboy for Caitlin #1253
Cattleman's Courtship #1306
Cattleman's Bride-to-Be #1457
Practice Makes Pregnant #1569
Cattleman's Heart #1605
The Prince's Bride #1640
Luke's Proposal #1745
Jesse's Child #1776
Chase's Promise #1791
Trey's Secret #1823
**The Princess and the Cowboy* #1865
†*Triple Trouble* #1957
Quinn McCloud's Christmas Bride #2007
††*Cinderella and the Playboy* #2036

*The McClouds of Montana
**The Hunt for Cinderella
†Fortunes of Texas: Return to Red Rock
††The Baby Chase

LOIS FAYE DYER

lives in a small town on the shore of beautiful Puget Sound in the Pacific Northwest with her two eccentric and lovable cats, Chloe and Evie. She loves to hear from readers. You can write to her c/o Paperbacks Plus, 1618 Bay Street, Port Orchard, WA 98366. Visit her on the Web at www.LoisDyer.com.

With my heartfelt thanks to Karen Edgel,
hospice nurse, in Republic, Washington.

Chapter One

"Hey, Jennifer—Dr. Demetrios just walked in."

Jennifer Labeaux noted her friend Yolanda's mischievous grin before she glanced over her shoulder. As usual, her heartbeat sped up at the sight of the tall, dark-haired male striding toward her section of the Coach House Diner.

Dr. Chance Demetrios was easily six feet four inches tall and built like a linebacker. He wore his black hair a shade long and his eyes were a deep chocolate brown—eyes that twinkled, charmed and seduced Jennifer with each conversation they shared.

She watched him slide into his usual booth, third from the back, with a view of the Cambridge, Massachusetts, street outside. He always sat in her section. Jennifer was torn between being flattered and wishing he wouldn't single her out. Not that she disliked him—quite the contrary. He made her yearn for things she knew she couldn't have and she was far too attracted to him for her own good. No doubt about it, Chance was too sexy, too rich and too high-octane for a waitress whose most sophisticated night out was visiting her neighborhood ice-cream shop with her five-year-old daughter.

Over the past six months, she'd seen Chance nearly every morning. There was no mistaking the male interest in his eyes but his persistent friendliness and good-natured acceptance of her refusals when he had asked her out had slowly but surely eased, and then erased, her natural wariness. The conversations she'd overheard between him and other customers only increased his appeal. He appeared to be genuinely interested in the lives of the diner regulars.

Even if dating were possible in her life at the moment, she'd never date Chance Demetrios, she thought with regret. Rumor had it that he loved women and went through girlfriends like a PMSing woman went through chocolate bars. Despite being powerfully attracted to him, Jennifer knew he was out of her league. If she ever became involved with a man again, he wouldn't be someone with a stable of women.

She tucked a menu under her arm, picked up a glass of ice water and a fresh pot of coffee and walked to the booth.

"Good morning, Dr. Demetrios," she said with a bright smile. "What can I get you?"

"Morning, Jennifer."

His deep voice seemed to linger over her name, sending shivers up her spine and heat curling through her belly.

Determined to ignore her rebellious body's reaction, Jennifer kept her gaze on the thick coffee mug as she poured. She steeled herself, setting down the pot and taking out her pad and pen. Despite preparing herself, however, meeting his gaze was a jolt. His dark eyes were warm, appreciative and filled with male interest.

And then he smiled. Jennifer had to fight to keep from melting into a pool of overheated hormones.

"The usual?" Thank goodness her voice didn't reflect her inner turmoil, she thought with relief and not a little surprise.

"Yeah, please," he said, his smile wry. "And maybe you can just hook up an IV with black coffee."

"Late night?" she asked with sympathy. Her gaze moved over his face, noting the lines of weariness she'd been too preoccupied to notice earlier. His dark eyes were heavy lidded and his jaw shadowed with beard stubble. He looked as if he'd either just rolled out of bed—or hadn't gone to bed at all. "Did you work all night?"

He shrugged. "Back-to-back emergency calls."

"You work too hard," she commented.

"All part of being a doctor." He smiled at her. "I knew the job had lousy hours when I signed on."

She lifted an eyebrow at his reasoning. "Maybe so, but if you don't sleep, how are you going to function?"

He glanced at the Rolex on his wrist. "Maybe I'll catch a nap on my office sofa before my first appointment."

"Good plan." Jennifer heard the cook call her name and realized she'd been chatting too long. "I have to go. I'll tell the other waitresses you need your coffee topped often this morning."

"Thanks."

Taken in by his appreciative smile, Jenny forced herself to nod pleasantly and turn to her next customer.

Through half-lowered lashes, Chance sipped the hot black coffee and watched her walk away. He suspected the employees and regulars in the diner weren't fooled by his attempts to play down his interest but he couldn't summon up the energy to care if they knew he loved looking at her. She wore the same attire as the rest of the waitresses—black slacks and white shirt under a black vest. But with her long legs, lush curls and graceful carriage, the clothes took on a different vibe on Jennifer. The diner's owner might think the uniform made his waitresses blend together, but she stood out like a long-stemmed rose in a bouquet of daisies.

He'd been asking her out for months now and each time, she'd turned him down. Six months earlier, he would have shrugged and moved on to the next beautiful woman. But for some reason that he couldn't begin to understand, he'd lost the urge to pursue other women since meeting Jennifer.

He couldn't accept that she wouldn't go out with him. He knew damn well she was attracted to him. Despite her never-wavering, cool-yet-friendly reserve, he felt the strong tug of sexual chemistry between them every time he saw her. He'd dated a lot of women over the years. He knew he hadn't misread the faint flush of color over the high arch of her cheekbones when they talked, nor the way she shielded her gaze with lowered lashes when he teased her.

No, Jennifer was definitely interested. But he'd asked her out at least a dozen times, probably more. She'd always refused, saying she didn't date customers.

From the snippets of conversation he'd overheard from the other waitresses, Chance didn't think she dated anyone at all.

Which only made him more intrigued and determined to spend time with her, away from the diner.

He rolled his shoulders to relieve the ache of muscles too long without rest and stretched his long legs out beneath the table. The red, vinyl-covered bench seat was comfortably padded and, like everything else in the Coach House Diner, reflected the 1950s theme. The effect was cheerful and welcoming. Chance had felt at home here from the first moment he'd stepped over the threshold six months earlier. Since the diner was only a short walk from the Armstrong Fertility Institute where he worked, it had quickly become his favorite place to have coffee, breakfast, lunch or grab a quick dinner if he'd worked late.

He glanced around the room, nodding at Fred, an elderly gentleman seated on a stool and eating his breakfast at the end of the long counter. Fred was a retired railroad engineer and, despite his advanced age of ninety-five, still woke early. Chance had spent more than one morning next to Fred on the round seats at the counter between 5:00 a.m. and 6:00.

He took another long sip of coffee and rubbed his eyes. It had been one hell of a week. After long hours of hard, frustrating work, he and his research partner Ted Bonner had finally disproved allegations that their work was questionable.

In the midst of proving the funding was legally and morally ethical, Chance had also watched as Ted fell in love and got married over the past several months. Chance would never admit it aloud, but observing his best friend's happiness had raised questions for Chance about his own lifestyle. Did he want to meet a woman who could make him settle down? Could he be monogamous?

Given his relationship history, Chance doubted it. He loved women—their smiles, their silky hair and skin, the way their eyes lit with pleasure when they made love.

No, he couldn't imagine ever settling down with one woman.

Which made him wonder why he hadn't dated anyone over the past six months.

Unconsciously, his gaze sought out Jennifer, locating her at the other end of the room. Her laughter pealed musically as she took an order from two women in business suits.

He muffled a groan and swigged down the rest of his coffee. He knew damn well Jennifer was the reason he hadn't dated anyone in months.

Or maybe I'm just too busy with work, he thought, unwilling to accept that the beautiful blonde was to blame for his nonexistent love life.

Midweek, he'd spent two long nights in the operating room. His volunteer work at a free clinic in a low-income Boston neighborhood often expanded to include surgery during emergency situations. This week, those emergencies seemed to roll in almost on each other's heels.

I'm too damn tired, he told himself. *That's why I'm being introspective. A solid eight hours of sleep and life will look normal again.*

He frowned at his empty coffee mug. He hated examining his feelings and no matter how he sliced it, he couldn't deny that he'd been spending too much time lately considering his life. And for a man who was rarely alone, he could swear he sometimes felt lonely.

"More coffee?"

Chance looked up. The red-haired waitress he often noticed talking with Jennifer stood next to his booth.

"Thanks."

She quickly filled his mug and left, letting Chance return to his brooding.

He'd had plenty of affairs, but none of his relationships with women could qualify as meaningful.

And that's the way I like it, he thought. *So why am I wondering if there ought to have been more?*

He dragged his hand over his face and rubbed his eyes. He reached into his jacket pocket but the tiny vial of nonprescription eyedrops he kept there was missing. Instead, he found a note he didn't remember putting there.

He scanned it and felt like groaning. The 3x5 card from his secretary was a reminder that the institute's annual Founder's Ball was the coming weekend.

And he didn't have a date. He frowned and tapped the card on the tabletop.

The prospect of going alone held no appeal. Attending the event was mandatory, and he'd *never* attend without a date.

What the hell, he thought. Given that the only pretty woman he wanted to date was Jennifer, he might as well bite the bullet and ask her to go with him.

She'll probably say no. She's never said yes any of the other times I've asked her out.

But just talking to her always made him smile— and he could use a smile this morning.

"Here you are—eggs over medium, French toast and bacon." Jennifer slid the plate onto the tabletop in front of him.

Perfect timing, he thought.

"Would you like me to bring you some aspirin?" she asked, glancing down sideways at him.

Her comment was so far from his thoughts that he blinked in confusion. "What? Why?"

"You were frowning as if your head hurt. I thought you might have a headache."

"Oh. No, I don't have a headache. Not yet, anyway." He held out the card. "I was reading this."

She glanced at the note, her eyes scanning the black type. "The Founder's Ball? It sounds very glamorous."

"It's black tie." His shrug spoke volumes about his lack of interest in whether the event was sophisticated. "The institute holds the ball every year. The band is supposed to be excellent and I hear the food's worth putting on a tux and tie—but it's no fun to go alone. Which is why you should take pity on me and be my date."

Jennifer brushed a strand of blond hair from her temple and fought the temptation to accept. The diner was located only a few blocks from the institute and many of its customers worked at the medical center.

The women employees had been buzzing about the Founder's Ball for weeks, discussing gowns, shoes, jewelry and hairstyles.

Enticing as it was to think about donning a glamorous dress to go dancing with Chance, however, she knew she couldn't.

"I'm sorry, but I can't." She slipped the card onto the table next to his hand, taking care not to let her fingers touch his. She'd made that mistake once and the shock of awareness that hit her when she'd brushed against him had rocked her. "Thank you for asking me, though."

"Don't thank me." His deep voice was almost a growl, although his dark eyes were rueful. "Just say yes."

She shook her head. "I told you. I never date customers."

He leaned back against the padded vinyl leather and tipped his head to the side, eyes narrowing consideringly over her. "What if I wasn't a customer?"

The question startled Jennifer and she laughed. "Too late. You're already a customer."

"So you don't date ex-customers, either?"

She shook her head.

"Damn."

"I have to get back to work," she told him, smiling

as he tipped his mug at her in salute before she turned and walked away.

"What's up with Dr. Hunk?" Yolanda asked the moment Jennifer joined her behind the long counter.

"I think he worked late last night," Jennifer responded, walking past her to the big coffee urn. She checked the levels and found one nearly empty so she measured ground coffee into a fresh paper filter.

"Is that all?" Yolanda joined Jennifer and leaned forward to peer into her face, her dark eyes assessing. "It looked like he was asking you out again."

"He did," Jennifer admitted.

"I hope you said yes this time."

"Of course not. You know I won't go out with a customer," Jennifer reminded her. She'd made up the rule on the spur-of-the-moment the first week she'd worked at the diner. To her surprise, the man who'd asked her out seemed to accept it with regret but little argument. She'd used the excuse several times since with the same results and no one had ever tempted her to change her mind—until Chance.

Yolanda rolled her eyes. "That's such a crock, Jennifer. You could make an exception." She glanced over her shoulder at the booth where Chance sat and sighed loudly. "Goodness knows, I certainly would for Dr. D."

Jennifer laughed. "Don't you think your husband might object?"

"Hmm. Good point." Yolanda's dimples formed as she grinned, her eyes flashing mischievously.

"Exactly," Jennifer said with emphasis. She tossed the used filter with its damp coffee grounds into the trash bin and slipped the new one into the big coffeemaker. "You'd have to say no, too, but for different reasons. The charming Dr. Demetrios will just have to find another Cinderella to take to the ball."

"To the ball?" Yolanda repeated, intrigued. "Do you mean, literally to a ball?"

"Actually, yes. He asked me to go to the Armstrong Fertility Institute Founder's Ball with him."

"What?" Yolanda's shriek drew the attention of the diners at the long counter behind them. She glanced at them, waved a hand to tell them to return to their bacon and eggs and focused on Jennifer. "Spill, girlfriend," she hissed. "I want details."

"That's all I've got," Jennifer protested. "He asked me to be his date for the Founder's Ball and I turned him down."

"I can't believe you refused a chance to go to that shindig. It's one of Boston's biggest parties!"

A third waitress joined them to collect a full coffeepot. Yolanda caught her sleeve. "Shirley, you're not going to believe this."

The red-haired woman paused, tucking her order pad into her pocket and eyeing Yolanda with interest. "What?"

"Dr. Demetrios asked Jennifer to go to the Founder's Ball with him—and she turned him down!"

Shirley's eyes widened. "Jennifer, you can't say no! There's no way Yolanda and I will ever get an invitation so you have to go, then come back and tell us all about it."

Jenny rolled her eyes. "I can't go out with Dr. Demetrios, Shirley. If I did, no one would ever again accept my I-don't-date-customers rule," Jennifer protested.

"Not if they don't know—so swear Dr. D to secrecy and make him promise not to tell anyone," Yolanda said promptly. "He's been trying to get you to go out with him for months—he'll swear not to tell anyone you broke your rule."

"Even if I wanted to go, I couldn't," Jennifer continued, trying a different argument. "The affair is black tie. I have nothing to wear—no dress, no shoes, no jewelry. It's not as if I can go in my best jeans."

Shirley dismissed the problem with a wave of her hand. "My best friend from high school is half owner of a high-end consignment shop. She can get you whatever you might need and it won't cost you a thing. She owes me a favor. I'll ask her to let us take everything home for the weekend and I'll return them on Monday morning before the shop opens. I'm sure she'll let us."

A fourth waitress joined them in time to hear Shirley's comments and her lively face lit with curiosity. "Who's getting a designer dress and jewelry?"

"Jennifer—Dr. D asked her to go to the Founder's Ball with him."

"No way!" Linda's eyes widened with surprise and delight. "Yeah, Jennifer! You're going, of course," she said with absolute conviction.

"I can't—you know I never date customers," Jennifer replied.

"Huh," Yolanda snorted. "You don't date. Period. I don't think you've gone out with anyone but the three of us since you started working here."

"That's true," Shirley conceded and nodded with firm agreement. "You've got to expand your horizons, Jennifer. Not that we don't love having you join us for outings after work and weekends, but honey—" she laid a hand on Jennifer's forearm and leaned closer, fixing her with a solemn gaze "—you seriously need to go out with a man."

"And get to know him—in the biblical sense," Linda added.

"I'm not hooking up with a guy for sex," Jennifer protested.

"Who said it was just for sex?" Yolanda countered. "The doc is the perfect guy for a weekend fling—he's nice, you've seen him nearly every day for the past six months so you can be sure he's not an ax murderer, he's interested in you and he has a reputation for never getting involved long-term with women." She ticked off her arguments one-by-one on the fingers of her right hand. "You'll have a great time and if you end up spending the weekend having great sex, well…that's just an added benefit. You've been living like a nun and Chance is the perfect man to end that state."

"I couldn't possibly spend the weekend with anyone," Jennifer protested, though she was shocked at how tempted she was by the idea.

She hadn't dressed up in an evening gown and attended a black-tie party since before her short-lived marriage to Patrick, her daughter's father. That Harvest Ball at the country club in her small Illinois hometown had been one of many such events, distinguished only because it had been the last dinner dance she'd attended before leaving for college.

A year later, she'd been married, divorced, and was six months pregnant with her little girl.

That was over five years ago and she hadn't worn a party dress, gone out on a date, nor slept with a man since. No wonder she was tempted, she thought. With an effort, she forced herself to focus on another reason to convince her friends she couldn't go to the Founder's Ball with Chance.

"And besides," she added, "I probably couldn't find a babysitter for Annie for an evening."

"That's absolutely not a problem," Linda assured her. "My kids would love to have her spend the week-end. Just yesterday they were asking when Annie was coming over again. We'll pick her up before your date and bring her home late Sunday afternoon."

Jennifer paused, staring at the trio of faces. Could she do this? More important, *should* she do this?

"Come on," Yolanda coaxed. "You know you want to."

"I shouldn't…" Jennifer began. She glanced over her shoulder and found Chance watching her, his dark eyes unreadable. The instant shiver of awareness was nothing new—he always elicited this response in her. He made her yearn, made her want.

Seeing his unfailing gentleness with elderly Mrs. Morgenstern when she routinely stopped him in the

diner to ask for medical advice had made Jennifer
sharply aware of the lack of a man's strength in her
own life. And the charm and dry wit with which he
deftly turned aside the inevitable passes from women,
all without hurting their feelings, made her wonder
if his reputation as a playboy was true. He seemed to
genuinely like women and go out of his way to be
kind, no matter their age or degree of beauty.

All of which only increased her attraction to him—
which made her more wary than ever. Her ex-husband
had been charming and handsome and she'd learned to
her sorrow that his goodness was a facade. Pretty words
and a handsome face had concealed a shallow, faith-
less heart. And after her bad experience with Patrick,
Jennifer questioned her own judgment when it came to
men. Everything about Chance drove her to obey the
urging of her body to give in and say yes. But how could
she be sure Chance was one of the good guys? Should
she give in just this once? Could she set aside her self-
imposed strict rules—and her role as responsible single
mother—and grab a few stolen hours of fun for herself?

"Go on, tell him yes," Shirley urged in a whisper
behind her.

Jennifer looked back at her friends. Their faces
held nearly identical expressions of encouragement
and affection.

"Are you sure you don't mind having Annie sleep over for the weekend?" she asked Linda.

"I'm positive!"

With sudden, uncharacteristic impulsiveness, Jennifer nodded abruptly. "Then I'll do it."

"Yes." Yolanda pumped her fist in the air and laughed.

Linda leaned closer. "Go tell him," she prodded in a whisper. "Right now." She caught Jennifer's shoulders and turned her around, giving her a little nudge toward the booth where Chance sat, frowning down at his mug of coffee.

Jennifer took a deep breath. She could hear her coworkers whispering as she walked away from them and couldn't suppress a smile. The three women were great friends and staunch supporters. She didn't doubt they were sincere when they'd told her they expected a full report on the institute's glamorous event—and every detail about her night out with the sexy doctor.

Chance looked up just as she reached his booth.

"If the invitation is still open, I'd love to go to the Founder's Ball with you," Jennifer said without preamble.

His mouth curved in a grin and Jennifer didn't miss the male satisfaction and what she thought was a gleam of triumph in his dark eyes.

"It's definitely still open."

"Good." She took her order pad and a pen from her pocket. "It's this weekend, isn't it? What time?"

"I'll pick you up at eight on Saturday. I need your address," he added.

"Right." She nodded, scribbled her street and apartment number on the back of an order slip, tore if off the pad and handed it to him. The slow, intimate smile he gave her sent a shiver of heated apprehension spiraling up her spine and she felt her cheeks warm. "Well." She cleared her throat. "I've got to get back to work."

"Absolutely."

"Then I guess I'll see you Saturday." She turned to walk away.

"Jennifer." The seductive deep drawl stopped her and she glanced at him over her shoulder. "Thanks for saying yes."

"You're welcome." She walked back to the counter, feeling his gaze between her shoulder blades like a caress. Fortunately, a customer stopped her and during their ensuing conversation, Chance paid his check and left the diner.

She wasn't comfortable knowing she was always aware of him on some level, she thought with stark honesty. Her senses appeared to be sharply tuned to him whenever he was around her. She felt his presence and departure like a tangible force each time he entered or left the diner. Pretending to ignore him hadn't solved the problem, nor had self lectures about the sheer stupidity of giving in to the attraction.

After her divorce, she'd vowed she wouldn't subject her daughter to a series of men friends rotating through their lives. Jennifer had spent her childhood watching substitute fathers move in and out of her mother's home after her parents' divorce. When the third very nice man moved on and her mother quickly fell in love with a fourth, Jennifer had stopped viewing any of her mother's boyfriends as permanent fixtures. Her mother was currently headed for divorce court for the sixth time.

Because Jennifer's grandparents were affluent, socially prominent members of the community, she'd never wanted for the necessities of food, clothing, good schools and a lovely home. But her life felt lonely and emotionally insecure. Lunch at the country club with her grandmother and piles of exquisitely wrapped presents under the Christmas tree didn't compensate for the lack of security under her mother's roof.

She'd married young while still in college and dreamed of a life filled with home and family. With stars in her eyes, she'd quit college to take a full-time job to support her husband, Patrick, a pre-med student. Six months after the wedding, she'd been devastated when Patrick was furious the night she told him she was pregnant. He'd accused her of lying about taking birth control pills and he moved out of their apartment within a week, immediately filing for divorce. He'd told her he needed a working wife whose first commitment was to him and he had no room in his life for a child. He'd even agreed to give her full custody and let her raise their baby alone since he had no interest in visitation rights. In return, she agreed not to request child support payments from him.

When he told their mutual friends that the divorce was Jennifer's choice, they reacted by ostracizing her and Jennifer was devastated. Much as she hated the snubs and vicious whisperings behind her back, however, she refused to be drawn into a mud-slinging match.

The divorce was final when Jennifer was six months pregnant. Three months later, she gave birth to Annie, a beautiful six-and-a-half-pound, red-haired baby girl with big blue eyes.

In the five years since Annie's birth, Jennifer had kept her vow to create a better life for her daughter than the one she'd known. She went to work, attended night classes to finish her college degree, and

spent her free time with her little girl. Men occasionally asked her out but she turned them down without
a single regret. If celibacy and a solo adult life was
the cost of giving Annie a secure, quiet life then it
was a small price to pay.

Jennifer knew her friends were convinced she
needed an adult social life, including a man to
share her bed. But she was committed to keeping
her vow to not repeat her mother's mistakes. She
swore her friends to silence, and they all promised
not to tell any interested men about Annie or other
details of her life. Fortunately, she hadn't met
anyone that stirred more than mild interest and
she'd certainly never considered sleeping with
anyone—until Chance walked into the diner and
smiled at her.

Since then, her sleep had been haunted by vivid
dreams of making love with him.

*Perhaps going out with him will get him out of my
system,* she thought.

Finishing her shift at two o'clock that afternoon,
Jennifer hurried home to collect her daughter from
the babysitter. She chatted for a few moments with
the spry seventy-eight-year-old Margaret Sullivan,
before she and Annie said goodbye and headed
across the hall to their own apartment. On the day

they'd moved in, Margaret had knocked on their door with a plate of warm cookies and a welcoming smile. When Jennifer's babysitter moved away, Margaret volunteered to have Annie stay with her while Jennifer worked or attended classes and the three had formed a close, familylike relationship.

"How was school today, Annie?" Jennifer asked when they were home in their own small kitchen. She filled the kettle at the sink and set it on the stove, switching on the burner.

"Fine," Annie replied as she carefully took three small plates from the lower cabinet next to the sink. "Me and Melinda are working on a project."

"Really? What kind of project?" Jennifer took two mugs from the cupboard. At the small corner table, Annie was carefully arranging four peanut butter cookies on one of the plates.

"We're building a miniature house with a kennel for our dogs." Annie shifted one of the cookies a bit to the left, eyed the plate critically, then nodded with approval. She looked up at Jennifer, her blue eyes glowing with fervor. "We're practicing for when we get our real dogs."

"I see." Jennifer caught her daughter in a quick hug, pressing a kiss against the silky red-gold curls. The teakettle whistled a warning and she released

Annie to turn off the burner. Pouring hot water into the mugs, she dropped an English Breakfast tea bag into hers and stirred hot chocolate mix into Annie's, then carried them over to the table. The little girl perched on a chair, legs swinging with enthusiasm. "You know, honey," Jennifer began, "it's going to be a while before we can have a dog." She set the gently steaming mug of chocolate in front of Annie and took the chair opposite.

"I know." Annie gave her mother a serene smile and stirred her drink with single-minded concentration.

"Not that I wouldn't like to have a dog, too," Jennifer continued. "But the landlord won't let us have pets in the apartment."

"It's all right, Mommy," Annie said. She sipped the chocolate from her spoon, made a small sound of satisfaction and drank from her mug. "I'm going to ask Santa for a dog this Christmas." She narrowed her eyes consideringly. "I think we need a house with a yard, too, don't you?"

"Uh…sure." Jennifer had no idea why Annie had decided that Santa would deliver a dog and a house by Christmas. *But it's only spring,* she thought, *and with luck, I can distract her and she'll forget about it by this winter.* Given that Annie had previously demonstrated a focused determination normally found in much older children, Jennifer wasn't convinced the delay would distract her daughter. Nevertheless, it was the only plan she had. "What did you and Melinda use to build your miniature house?"

Jennifer's attempt to distract Annie worked as the little girl launched into an enthusiastic description of the two shoe boxes they'd taped together and how they'd used scissors to cut out dog photos from a magazine.

The mugs were half-empty before Annie's recital of the day's events was exhausted. Jennifer eyed her over the rim of her tea mug and smiled as her daughter broke off a chunk of peanut butter cookie and tucked it neatly into her mouth.

"I have a surprise for you, Annie," she said. "How would you like to have a sleepover at Jake and Suzie's house this weekend?"

"Oooh, yes!" Annie bounced in her chair, her eyes lit with excitement. "May I take my backpack and my Lilia-Mae doll and my Enchanted Pony so Suzie and I can play with them?"

"Yes, of course." Jennifer laughed when Annie jumped off her chair and threw herself into her mother's arms, climbing into her lap as she listed all the many things she wanted to take with her.

Jennifer felt a stab of misgiving as she cuddled the

warm, vibrant little body in her arms. This quiet apartment with Annie was her real life and she loved it—a world filled with her beautiful little girl and her busy days with work and college classes. A date with Chance Demetrios—at the ritzy Founder's Ball, no less—was a huge step outside the constraints of the life she'd built.

But her friends were right, too, she realized. Sometimes, she was lonely and longed for an emotional—and physical—connection with a partner. There was no room for a permanent man in her life just now and wouldn't be for the foreseeable future. But just for one night, perhaps it wouldn't do any harm if she seized the opportunity to play Cinderella before returning to the quiet rhythm of her busy days with Annie.

Jennifer rested her cheek against her daughter's silky red-gold curls, breathed in her little-girl smell of shampoo, soap and crayons, and contentedly listened to Annie's excited plans for spending the weekend with her friends.

Chance hadn't recognized the street address that Jennifer had scribbled on the note after she had accepted his invitation so he'd made a mental note to check it out later. He tucked the paper safely away in his pocket until later that evening, when he turned on his laptop to browse the Internet. It took his computer only a few moments to search, find a street map of Boston and pinpoint Jennifer's neighborhood.

He frowned at the screen, trying to visualize the area. He thought her apartment might be located within a mile or two of the free clinic where he volunteered. He typed in a request for directions from his own town house, in an upscale Boston neighborhood, to Jennifer's address. The resultant map details confirmed his guess that her street wasn't more than a short cab drive and probably within walking distance from the free clinic. The two addresses were in a shabby though respectable area of Boston, not far from his own home in actual miles but light-years away in real-estate prices.

Chance didn't give a damn that Jennifer's address highlighted the disparity in their incomes but it drove home the fact that he knew little about her life away from the diner.

He'd noticed her sitting in a back booth to study on her coffee breaks at the diner and when he'd commented, she'd told him that she was taking college classes. But beyond being a student and working as a waitress, she was an enigma to him. He wondered if she lived alone or shared an apartment with a fellow student.

During their brief conversations, she'd never mentioned her family and he realized that he didn't know if she had any sisters or brothers, or if her parents lived here in Boston. He couldn't help but wonder what her childhood had been like, what kind of a family she came from, and where she'd grown up. Jennifer treated Mrs. Blake, the elderly widow who counted out coins to pay for her daily coffee and donut, with the same friendly respect that she gave to the head of the Armstrong Fertility Institute. He'd never seen her react as if any of the high-powered doctors or scientists who frequented the diner intimidated her in the slightest.

Which made him think she must have grown accustomed to dealing with powerful, influential people before she arrived at the Coach House Diner.

She didn't seem to recognize the Demetrios name, however, which indicated to him that while her family may have been affluent, they didn't move in his parents' stratified circle. The Demetrios shipping empire had made his family very, very rich and by definition, made him heir to an obscenely large fortune. Chance knew his father felt he'd turned his back on the family business when he chose to become a doctor. The choice had driven a wedge between him and his parents, especially his father.

Much as he loved them, however, he couldn't ignore the deep, passionate commitment he felt to medicine.

He wondered if Jennifer's parents were happy with her career choice of waitress and part-time college student.

Which brought him full circle, he realized, to the fact that he was apparently bewitched by every facet of the mysterious Miss Labeaux.

That there was much he didn't know about the beautiful blonde only made her more intriguing. Anticipation curled through his midsection.

I'll find out Saturday night, he reflected.

Chapter Two

At seven-fifteen on Saturday night, Jennifer was well on her way to being transformed into Cinderella. Linda, Yolanda and Shirley had knocked on her door at 5:00 p.m., laden with bags. They'd dropped boxes, bags and bottles atop her bed before they raided her kitchen for wineglasses. After pouring wine and setting out a tray of crackers and cheese on her dresser, they had shooed her into the shower.

She had shampooed and scrubbed with Linda's gift of plumeria-scented gel before toweling off and smoothing the matching floral lotion over her skin.

She had heard Annie's giggles over the throb of music from the radio on her bedside table and when she had pulled on her robe and left the bathroom, she had found Annie dancing with Yolanda. The two had twirled and spun in the small carpeted space at the foot of the bed while they sang along with a 1980s disco song.

Their enthusiasm had far outweighed their vocal talents and Jennifer had laughed as the song ended with a flourish.

Jennifer replayed the fresh memories just made over the past hour. "Hi, Mommy." Annie left Yolanda and wrapped her arms around Jennifer's waist, dimples flashing in her flushed face as she grinned up at her. "We're disco dancing."

"I see that," Jennifer told her. "Very impressive."

"But now I have to dry your mom's hair," Yolanda said, handing Jennifer a glass of wine and motioning her to have a seat on a chair she'd placed at the end of the bed. "We'll dance more later, okay, Annie?"

"Okay," the little girl agreed promptly. She curled up on the bed and settled in to watch as Yolanda worked on Jennifer's damp hair.

Yolanda wielded blow dryer and curling iron with expertise and a half hour later, stood back to eye Jennifer.

"Perfect," she declared with satisfaction.

"Will you do my hair next, Yolanda?" Annie asked, gathering fistfuls of red-gold curls and bunching a handful of the silky mass on each side of her head.

"Absolutely, kiddo." Yolanda grinned at her. "Shirley's going to help your mom with her makeup in the bathroom. You can take her place over here."

Jennifer left Annie chattering away as Yolanda French-braided her long curls. In the bathroom, Shirley upended a brocade bag of makeup onto the small countertop and lined up pots of eyeshadow, brushes for the loose powder, several tubes of lipstick and a handful of lip color pencils.

Jennifer heard Annie chattering and laughing with Yolanda as she applied makeup and Shirley offered advice. At last, she slicked lush color on her lips and smoothed clear gloss over the deep red lipstick, then stood back to critically view the effect.

The mauve eyeshadow turned her eyes a deeper blue, smoky and mysterious, set within a thicket of dark lashes. Subtle rose color tinted her cheeks. She tilted her head, loving the soft brush of silky blond curls against her nape and temples.

"Perfect," Shirley pronounced, standing behind her. Their gazes met in the mirror. "Just perfect. You look fabulous, girlfriend. Time to get dressed."

"Ahem." Jennifer loudly cleared her throat and struck a pose in the doorway.

"Ooh, Mommy." Annie's awestruck voice reflected the delight shining in her widened blue eyes. "You look just like a princess."

"Thank you, sweetheart." Jennifer caught her daughter close, receiving a tight hug in return. "Now you have to scoot," she said, giving her one last hug before looking down at her. "Be good for Linda, okay? And have fun."

"I will." Annie twirled away to grab her backpack. "I'll tell you all about it when I come home on Sunday."

"I can't wait," Jennifer assured her solemnly, exchanging a glance with Linda that shared a wry understanding, one mother to another.

Fifteen minutes later, Jennifer waved goodbye from the window as her friends climbed into their cars on the street below. Annie and Linda paused to wave up at her and moments later, the brake lights of Linda's blue sedan disappeared around the corner at the end of the block.

After the laughter, chatter and teasing advice of her friends, the apartment seemed too quiet with only the radio for company. The air in the room felt hushed and expectant, as if the place itself was waiting. Jennifer swept the neat living room with a quick glance before walking into her bedroom to collect the satin wrap that matched her dress.

Turning to leave, she caught a glimpse of her reflection in the long mirror mounted on the back of her bedroom door. Jennifer paused—the woman staring back at her seemed like a stranger. The scarlet gown fit as if custom-sewn for her alone. It had a square neckline, cut low across the swell of her breasts, with tiny cap sleeves and a bodice that hugged her narrow waist. The skirt was made up of yards of floating chiffon and lace and the toes of red, strappy high heels peeked from beneath the hem.

She wore her few pieces of good jewelry—three narrow gold bangle bracelets inset with tiny diamonds and small diamond studs in the lobes of her ears. Around her neck she wore her silver locket with Annie's picture. She knew it didn't quite match, but she'd never taken it off. Yolanda had pinned her caramel-blond curls atop her head in a soft upsweep that left the line of her throat bare, but wisps curled down her neck at the back.

The designer dress truly made her feel like Cinderella, waiting for the Prince to take her to the ball. The fanciful thought made her smile as she thought ruefully of her date's playboy reputation.

A knock sounded on the outer door and Jennifer froze. Butterflies fluttered in her stomach and she pressed the flat of her hand to her abdomen, drawing a deep breath and reaching for calmness. Then she quickly left the bedroom and crossed the living room where a cautious glance through the hall door's peephole sent her heartbeat racing once again. She drew another deep breath, slowly exhaled and opened the door.

Chance stood just outside in the hallway. He wore a classic black tuxedo, a white formal shirt fastened with onyx studs, a black bow tie and polished black dress shoes. She'd thought him handsome in casual jeans and leather jacket, but she realized helplessly that he was undeniably heart-stopping in formal wear. His gaze swept over her from head to toe and back again without the slightest attempt to conceal his interest.

"Hello." His deep voice drew out the word, the raspy growl loaded with undercurrents.

"Hello." Jennifer felt the brush of his gaze and desire curled, heating her skin, making it tingle with awareness.

"Ready to go?" Chance asked. He hadn't missed her reaction to his slow appraisal and the throb of arousal beat through his veins as he watched a faint flush move up her throat to tint her cheeks. She lowered her lashes, concealing her eyes.

"I just need to collect my purse." She left him to cross the room.

He watched her walk away, his gaze intent on the gown's long skirt. It swayed with each step, outlining the feminine curve of her hips and thighs with tantalizing briefness. The nape of her neck and the pale skin of her back to just above her narrow waist was bare, framed by crimson lace and a few loose curls. She disappeared through a doorway, momentarily releasing him from the spell that held him.

His gaze skimmed the room. The apartment was as neat as the rest of the old, well-maintained building and Jennifer's living space held a warmth that was missing in his professionally decorated town house. A blue and cream-colored afghan draped over one arm of a white-painted wood rocking chair that sat at right angles to an overstuffed blue sofa. A framed poster of the New York Metropolitan Museum of Art hung on the wall above the sofa. At the far end of the room, a bookcase was stuffed with hardcovers and paperbacks, the overflow stacked in a bright pile at one end. Chance resisted the urge to walk closer and inspect the titles on the spines, curious to learn what she read. A television and DVD player took up the two shelves on a low cabinet against one wall and beyond, a kitchen area boasted a white-painted table with four chairs pushed up to it. A bright blue cloth runner ran down the center while a small stack of notebooks and what looked like a thick textbook were spread out over one end.

Just as he was about to step over the threshold, drawn inexorably by the rooms that he instinctively knew would give him a deeper insight into Jennifer, she reappeared.

"Got everything?" he asked as he watched her walk toward him. Heat stirred in his gut, just as it did each time he saw her at the diner.

"Yes." She stepped into the hall, turning briefly to lock the door before they moved toward the elevator.

Outside, the spring night was slightly chilly and Jennifer draped the long satin wrap around her shoulders and throat. She tossed one crimson end over her shoulder and let it drape down her back, covering her bare shoulder blades above the gown's skirt.

"Cold?" Chance asked as he keyed the lock and opened the door of a sleek black Jaguar sedan parked at the curb.

"Just a little," Jennifer murmured, sliding into the low seat.

"I'll turn the heater on in a second." Chance bent to tuck her skirt out of the way and closed the door.

A moment later, he slid into the driver's seat beside her.

Jennifer fastened her seat belt and stroked her fingertips over the butter-soft leather of the seat. Her gaze swept the compact, luxurious interior. "Nice car," she said, breathing in the faint scent of leather and men's cologne.

"Thanks." Chance grinned at her and winked. "I like it." His fingers moved over a series of buttons on the dash and heated air brushed Jennifer's toes. The seat warmed beneath her. "How's that?" he asked.

"Lovely." She smiled at him, feeling distinctly cosseted.

"Good—let me know if you want it warmer." He glanced in the mirrors, shifted into gear and the Jag pulled smoothly away from the curb.

"Where is the ball being held?" Jennifer inquired as they left her block and headed downtown.

"Same place as last year, apparently," Chance replied with a sideways glance and named a posh hotel that was fairly new but built in a traditional turn-of-the-century style. It had become an instant Boston landmark, its dining room and ballrooms favored by society mavens.

"I've never been there," Jennifer said, intrigued. "But I read an article in the *Boston Herald* about the grand opening. The design alone sounded fabulous."

"Rumor has it the financier was a mad count from Austria who was a distant relative of Dracula."

"What?" Jennifer's gaze flew to his. His dark eyes were lit with amusement. "You're joking."

"Nope." He raised his hand, palm out. "I swear someone actually told me that."

"And did you believe them?" Jennifer asked with a laugh.

"Not a word."

"Excellent," she responded promptly. "I'm glad to know you're a sensible man."

"Oh, I'm sensible," he replied. "Now if you'd said I was a 'nice, safe' guy, I would have had to rethink my answer."

She shot him a chastening look from beneath her lashes and found his mouth curved in a half smile that set awareness humming through her torso. "Hmm," she said. "I don't think I'll ask you why." With an abrupt change of subject, she pointed out the window. "Isn't that the hotel?"

Chance lifted a brow and his gaze met hers for a brief moment before he nodded, downshifting as he turned out of traffic and drove beneath the portico.

The lobby was a fascinating blend of old and new, with jewel-toned, blown-glass Chihuly light fixtures hanging from boxed ceilings. A broad expanse of thick black and gold carpeting covered the floors, and round seats upholstered in gold were arranged at intervals between the reception desk and the wide hallway on their left.

Jennifer loosened her wrap from her throat and let it slip down her arms to catch at her elbows. Chance took her hand and tucked it through the bend of his arm, the move securing her against his side.

She didn't shift away from the press of his body against hers although she had the feeling she was playing with fire. She was all too aware of his reputation with women; in fact, she'd overheard several diner conversations about the subject between female employees from the institute. She didn't doubt that Chance had plans for ending the evening with her in his bed. Which left only one question—did she want the same thing?

She was certainly attracted to him. She also knew that their conversations over the past six months had led to her feeling more than just physically drawn to him. Still, she wasn't sure if she wanted more from this evening than the sheer pleasure of an adult night out with a handsome man. And since she *was* undecided, she told herself to stop worrying and simply enjoy the party.

Chance led her down the wide hallway, one side lined with upscale shops. Some were filled with jewelry and designer clothing while several stores resembled Aladdin's cave, aglow with colorful glassware and gifts. Directly across from the shops was a long bank of elevators.

"Going up?" a man called, holding the door of a half-filled car.

"Yes, thanks," Chance told him, handing Jennifer ahead of him into the elevator.

They shifted to the rear of the car as three other couples entered and Jennifer found herself standing in front of Chance. When the elevator stopped on the next floor up and several other people entered, the crowd shifted backward once again, compressing the free space even farther.

Jennifer stepped nearer to Chance to avoid being bumped by the large man in front of her and Chance slipped his arm around her waist, pulling her closer and into the shelter of his body. By necessity, however, the move brought her bare back flush against his chest, his arm a warm bar across her midriff.

She felt surrounded by him. Each breath she took drew in the faint scent of his cologne and shifted the texture of his black jacket against her mostly bare arms, pressed the round black shirt studs against her waist.

She closed her eyes, flooded by sensations as her awareness of him intensified. She wanted to sink against his powerful body, wanted to pull his arms closer and wrap them around her, but instead, she forced her eyes open. And caught her breath when she gazed directly into the mirrored elevator wall and the reflection of Chance's heavy-lidded eyes. Heat flooded her, matching the burn in his dark stare.

She stood still and his hand tightened at her waist, muscles flexing in the hard body that held her close. The moment was taut with silent tension. She nearly groaned with frustration when the connection was abruptly broken by the ping of the elevator when it came to a smooth stop. The doors opened with an audible whoosh, the sound further shattering the moment.

"Our floor," Chance murmured in her ear, his voice deeper, rougher.

Jennifer didn't reply, unsure if her voice would actually function. She and Chance moved with the crowd, conversation unnecessary amid the laughter and chatter. Chance's hand rested at the small of her back, a warm weight that tied her to him as surely as if it were an invisible chain.

Never had she been so conscious of the differences between male and female, nor so compelled to explore the undeniable pull on her senses that drew her inexorably toward him.

They reached a wide archway and the guests around them slowed, forming a straggling line as they waited to enter the dining room.

"Dinner should be great," Chance murmured. "I happen to know one of the chefs." He took a square, gold-embossed, cream-colored card from his inner jacket pocket as the line moved forward.

"Good evening, Dr. Demetrios." The tuxedo-clad man standing just outside the door smiled with warmth, nodding at Jennifer. "Ma'am."

"Hello, Frank," Chance replied. "Tell your boss I'm glad he's doing the catering tonight. I was seriously considering skipping the dinner until I heard he was the chef."

"I'll tell him." The man's smile broadened. He took the invitation from Chance and consulted a seating chart. "You and your lady are with the senator and his wife at a front table." He snapped his fingers and a waiter instantly appeared. "Joseph, show the doctor and his guest to table number four."

"Yes, sir. This way, please." The young man

sketched a quick, respectful nod and led the way across the room.

Jennifer tried not to stare as they crossed the beautifully appointed art-deco dining room. White linen tablecloths covered round tables, each set for eight guests with polished silverware, gold-trimmed china, sparkling crystal glasses and fresh floral centerpieces. Crystal chandeliers were spaced at intervals down the ceiling and glittered and gleamed, adding their brilliance to the recessed lighting in the boxed ceiling.

"Chance!" A tall man with a mane of white hair and sun lines fanning from the edges of shrewd blue eyes stood as they reached a table just to the left of the speaker's podium. "I told Emily Armstrong to make sure we sat at your table. I'm glad it worked out."

"Hello, Archie." Chance shook the man's outstretched hand before draping an arm over Jennifer's shoulder. "Jennifer, this is Senator Claxton and his wife, Evelyn. Their son, Ben, was my best friend from kindergarten through college. Archie and Evelyn, this is Jennifer Labeaux."

"Good evening," Jennifer held out her hand and received a firm, warm handshake.

"Glad to meet you, Jennifer," the senator said, his eyes kind, his smile welcoming.

Seated on his left, his wife nodded and smiled. "It's nice to meet you, dear." The silver-haired woman leaned forward. "We must make a pact to keep Archie and Chance from talking politics or funding for medical research all during dinner. When they get started, they argue for hours."

"Then we definitely need to divert them," Jennifer told her as she slipped into the chair Chance held. "You lead, I'll follow."

"Excellent." Evelyn nodded with approval.

"Now, Evie," her husband protested as he and Chance settled into their seats. "I don't know how you can object to a little friendly discussion, especially since tonight is a fundraiser for the institute and it's one of your pet projects."

"Oh, I certainly want to raise money for research," Evelyn said serenely. "I just don't want you and Chance to spend all evening discussing nothing but political funding. Especially when there's bound to be so many other interesting subjects to talk about tonight. Like for instance," she continued as she tilted her head, her voice lowering, "the not-quite-divorced starlet who just walked in on the arm of a certain land-development billionaire. Don't stare!" She caught the sleeve of her husband's tuxedo jacket to keep him from turning to look.

"Shoot, Evie," the senator grumbled. "How do you expect me not to react when you hit me with one of your bombshells?"

"I'm continually amazed at the depth of your knowledge about society's movers and shakers and the gossip they stir up," Chance teased. He lounged in his seat, one arm resting across the gold-trimmed back of Jennifer's chair. His fingers moved lazily, brushing her arm just below the edge of her capped sleeve. Goose bumps lifted in the wake of his touch.

"A senator's wife has to have something to occupy her while her husband is off doing governmental things," the older woman told him. "I just happen to have access to a very well-informed network of gossips." She winked at Jennifer.

Jennifer laughed, charmed by the couple. Before she could respond, however, two other couples arrived to take their seats at the table and there was an ensuing flurry of introductions and conversation.

She felt as if she'd been dropped back in time to the country club in her hometown. The Claxtons reminded her of a couple who had been longtime friends of her grandparents and their comfortable, loving repartee had her laughing out loud along with Chance. They clearly adored Chance, too, which

Jennifer took as an endorsement of her growing conviction that he was definitely one of the good guys.

One of the other couples at the table had a four-year-old daughter and Jennifer had to make a conscious effort to keep from sharing stories about Annie at that age. The husband was a TV producer and his wife was a local Boston news anchor. Jennifer often watched her on the late-night broadcast and was delighted to learn that she was every bit as nice in person as she seemed on television.

When dinner—which was truly delicious—was finished, the doors were opened into the adjoining ballroom. Lush music filled the high-ceilinged room from the orchestra seated on a dais, edged with potted palms, at the far end of the polished floor.

Shoulder propped against the wall, his hands thrust into his pockets, Chance waited at the edge of the ballroom while Jennifer disappeared into the ladies' room.

"Hey, Chance."

The tap on his shoulder had him straightening from the wall. Behind him were Paul Armstrong and his siblings Derek and Lisa.

"Evening, everybody," Chance smiled at the twin brothers and winked at the petite, dark-haired Lisa. The two men wore traditional black tuxedos with pristine white shirts and bow ties, while Lisa's dress was clearly a designer gown, the oyster-and-bronze-colored dress held up by a collar of jewels. It left her back and shoulders bare and Chance reflected idly that both she, and her brothers, looked every bit the society powerhouses they were. "This is quite a party."

"Yes, it is, isn't it?" Lisa said with a smile of satisfaction, her gaze sweeping over the crowded ballroom. "Everyone seems to be having a good time."

"I'd say so," Chance agreed. He flagged down a passing waiter and took champagne flutes from the tray, handing one to each of the Armstrongs. "Congratulations, you three. I'm guessing the institute's coffers will grow after tonight."

Chance lifted his glass in salute and they all sipped.

"Is the whole family here?" He glanced past the trio to briefly scan the crowd for their sister and her husband. "I don't think I've seen Olivia and Jamison."

"Oh, yes, they're here," Lisa assured him. "We were just talking with them."

"Yeah," Paul said with a shake of his head. "They were telling us about their adoption plans."

"Adoption plans?" Chance echoed, surprised. "I didn't know they were thinking of adopting a child."

"Children—plural," Derek told him. "Two brothers. The younger one is autistic."

"Really?" Chance wasn't sure what to say. Adopting an autistic child was a noble action but a very big challenge for the parents—especially when one parent was a busy junior senator with one eye on the White House. "That's quite an undertaking."

"I agree," Lisa said, worry underlying her tone. "I can't help but wonder if they're truly prepared for the impact of a special-needs child in their lives."

"I think Olivia is determined," Paul said with a shrug. "Only time will tell but my money's on her and Jamison."

"Excuse me, sir." A woman, carrying a clipboard and wearing a unobtrusive "Staff" button on her green evening gown, interrupted them with an apologetic look. "Senator Claxton would like to introduce all of the Armstrong family members to a friend of his." She lowered her voice to murmur, "The senator asked me to tell you the friend is a potential donor to the research program at the institute."

Derek slipped his arm through Lisa's and clapped Paul on the shoulder. "Then we'd better go meet-and-greet."

"Duty calls. See you later, Chance." Paul let his brother urge him into motion.

"Have fun," Lisa called over her shoulder as the three followed the clipboard-carrying woman into the throng.

Chance lifted his half-empty flute in farewell.

"Who are they?" Jennifer asked, having returned in time to see the Armstrongs leave.

Her voice stroked over his senses, lush, sensual, and when he turned, the sight of her did the same.

"My bosses—and coworkers," he answered, dismissing them with a wave of the champagne class before deftly depositing the flute on a passing waiter's tray. "They were called away to meet potential donors. For them tonight is both business and pleasure. I'd like you to meet them—hopefully we'll see them later and I'll introduce you." He held out his hand. "Dance with me?"

She smiled shyly. "I'd love to."

Chance swept Jennifer onto the floor. They circled the room amid the crowd of dancers, moving gracefully to the strains of a waltz.

"I feel like Cinderella," Jennifer murmured.

Chance tucked her closer, his leg brushing between hers as he executed a turn. "Does that make me the prince?" he asked.

She tilted her head back to look up at him. "I'm not sure," she said. "I think the jury's still out."

"Damn." His smile was wry. "And I've been on my best behavior tonight."

His eyes twinkled, inviting her to laugh.

"After listening to you and the senator tell stories about the pranks you and his son pulled on your friends in school, I'm not sure you grasp the concept of 'good behavior,'" she teased.

"Isn't there a statute of limitations on being a dumb kid? Dave and I did most of that stuff in high school and college," he protested.

"Nothing recently?" she pressed with a smile, unconvinced.

"No," he assured her. "We had a lot of fun in school but my days of setting up practical jokes are over. I wish I had time to see more of the senator's family," he added. "But for the past few years, Ted and I have been too busy with our research."

Her gaze softened. "You work too hard. Lately when you come into the diner, you seem exhausted."

"There have been a few weeks when sleep was a rare commodity," he admitted.

"What exactly do you do at the institute?" she asked, insatiably curious about every aspect of his life.

"I treat women with fertility issues," he told her. "Part of my day is spent with patients in one-on-one appointments and procedures. The rest of the day is spent in the lab with my partner. We're searching for a way to increase the success rate of implanted embryos, among our other projects."

"That's marvelous." Jennifer couldn't help but think about how difficult it must be for couples who wanted children but couldn't conceive. Annie was the most important thing in her life—what if she couldn't have gotten pregnant? "I can't imagine doing anything more important."

"That's how I feel. How I've always felt." His voice deepened, eyelashes half-lowering over dark eyes. "You understand and you've only known me a few months. I started bandaging the neighborhood dogs when I was eight years old but my parents still can't understand why I want to be a doctor."

"Why not?" Baffled, she searched his features. "Most parents would love to have a doctor in the family."

"They wanted me to go into the family business. My father especially. He's the CEO and he wanted me to take his place." He shrugged. "If they'd had more children, it might have been easier for them to accept my decision but unfortunately I'm an only child."

"It must have been difficult for you to disappoint them," she murmured in response to the hint of regret underlying his words.

"Yeah," he admitted. "It was—still is, sometimes."

"But you love your work so it's worth it to you," she guessed.

"Yes." He smiled at her, his dark eyes warm. "How about you? Do you like working at the diner?"

"I do," Jennifer replied. "I like the customers, the other waitresses, even my boss. I plan to keep working there until I get my degree."

"What are you studying?"

"Education—I want to be a teacher."

"Good for you." His smile held approval and respect. "What kind of classes are you taking?"

"An English lit class, which I love," she told him. "And a psychology class, which I don't like very much. Still," she added, "at least it's not an art class."

"You don't like art?"

"Oh, I love art," she assured him. "I love going to museums and looking at sculpture, oil paintings, watercolors…I especially love Impressionist paintings. But I have very little artistic talent, unfortunately, and I need a passing grade in several art classes to finish my degree."

"How many hours are you at the diner every week?" he asked with a frown. "Aren't you working full-time? How do you have time to study?"

She smiled impishly. "I don't date. It's amazing

how much free time a woman has when she cuts men out of her life."

His arms tightened, pulling her closer. "That's got to change," he growled.

She laughed, her breasts pressed to the muscled strength of his chest, his powerful thighs hard against hers. Excitement and heat shivered through her and she tilted her head back to look up at him. "But I have to earn my degree if I want to become a teacher—and I really, really want to be a teacher."

His gaze studied her before he nodded. "I can see you being a teacher—little kids, right? Or are you thinking of teenagers?"

She shook her head. "I'm more interested in grade school."

"Yet another thing we have in common," he commented. "Both of us want careers where we can help people."

She stared into his eyes, struck by the truth of his comment. They did seem to have a lot in common—and with each new revelation, her feelings for him deepened.

Conversation lapsed as they danced, the brush of their bodies casting a spell that held them, growing stronger, hotter with each movement of body against body as they swayed to the music.

When the orchestra took a break, Chase tipped his head back to look down at her.

"Thirsty?"

Jennifer nodded and Chance released her, his hand stroking in a warm caress down her arm before he threaded her fingers through his and led her from the crowded dance floor.

Guests strolled the periphery of the ballroom, sat with wineglasses at small tables, or gathered in groups to chat and observe the colorful swirl of other guests in the center of the room.

The champagne fountain sat on a white linen-covered table. Chance handed a filled crystal flute to Jennifer and lifted a second one.

"Hello, Chance. Frank told me you were here."

Jennifer looked over her shoulder, her eyes widening at the lanky, blond man in a white chef's coat. His features were movie-star handsome and a counterpoint to Chance's dark masculinity.

"Jordan," Chance greeted him with a wide grin. The two men shook hands and then Chance slipped his free hand around Jennifer's waist to draw her closer. "Jennifer, this is Jordan Massey, the best chef in Boston."

"Pleased to meet you, Jennifer." The swift glance Jordan raked over her was pure male interest.

Jennifer felt a subtle tension in Chance. The possibility that he might be jealous of the good-looking chef was intriguing but she dismissed the notion. Instead, she smiled and held out her hand. "It's lovely to meet you, Jordan. I'm so glad I have an opportunity to tell you how wonderful our dinner was—I can't remember when I've enjoyed a meal more."

"Thank you." He took her hand, holding it a second too long and giving her fingers a light squeeze before releasing her. He lifted an eyebrow at Chance. "She's beautiful and she loves my cooking. Where have you been hiding her, Chance?"

"Never mind." Chance's voice held a definite possessive warning. "Back off."

Jordan laughed and winked at Jennifer. "Duty and my kitchen calls but we'll have to talk later, Jennifer, and you can tell me how you've managed to make my friend so possessive."

"I'm just protecting her from the wolves," Chance drawled.

"Of course," Jordan said blandly. "Enjoy the evening, my friend."

Jennifer didn't miss the enigmatic look he gave Chance before he disappeared into the crowd.

"Where did you meet him?" she asked Chance, curious about the chef.

"His sister was a patient of mine," he told her. "He threw a party when the baby was born and after everyone else went home, we killed a fifth of Scotch toasting his new niece. We've been friends ever since."

She sipped her champagne, her gaze drifting over the glittering gathering before stopping on a couple. The man wore a tux and the woman's gown was a formfitting sapphire blue, her hair a long, wavy mane that gleamed like silk beneath the chandelier's light. The two had eyes only for each other—until the man glanced up, grinned and waved.

"There's Ted," Chance commented, lifting his champagne glass in salute.

"Who's the woman with him?" Jennifer asked.

"His wife," Chance replied. "And I'm damned grateful Sara Beth said yes when he proposed. I work with him and he's been a pain in the…well, let's just say he was in a bad mood until he worked things out with her."

"They look very much in love," Jennifer said softly, her gaze on the two as the man brushed the woman's long wavy hair over her shoulder and smiled down at her.

"They are." Chance emptied his champagne flute and caught her hand. "Let's dance." He deposited their glasses. "I'm glad to know I was right," he said as they circled the room.

"About what?" she asked, a tiny frown drawing her brows into a vee.

"The food," he replied easily as he guided her out through open French doors and onto the wide balcony where other guests danced beneath the night sky. "Unless you were lying to Jordan. You did enjoy dinner?"

Her brow smoothed and a smile curved her mouth, lighting her eyes. "Oh, yes. The lobster was wonderful and the chocolate mousse was perfect."

"I told you the food would be worth the cost of the ticket," he said with satisfaction, executing a series of smooth, sweeping turns to move them down the length of the wide stone balcony. "Jordan doesn't serve tiny slivers of artsy-looking food. His food is elegant without being precious—you know, no tiny portions that leave a guy so hungry that he has to stop for a burger on his way home."

Jennifer looked up at him, a smile curving her lips. "It sounds suspiciously as if you've been forced to sit through dinners filled with…maybe, cucumber sandwiches and tea?"

He laughed. "Not since my grandmother made me eat them when I was a kid. Since then, though,

I've had to attend dinners where we were served rubbery chicken or tiny plates with three or four artfully arranged celery and radish slices." He shuddered. "Makes me hungry just to think of it."

"I'm guessing it takes more than celery and radishes to fuel a guy your size," she joked.

"You guess right," he said with a nod. "Lots more. I have a big appetite." He winked at her.

She studied him, contemplating an answer to what was clearly an invitation.

His lips brushed her ear. "Aren't you wondering what other appetites I have?" he teased, lazy amusement underlaid with darker, more volatile emotions.

She tilted her head and his mouth brushed over her cheek, with scant inches separating his lips from hers. "I was considering asking," she said quietly. "But decided I should give the subject more thought before asking questions that might provoke dangerous answers."

"I'd be happy to answer any questions, Jennifer," he told her. "Dangerous or not." Heat flared in his dark, heavy-lidded gaze.

"I've never been a woman who courts danger," she murmured. "I've always preferred safe and sane."

"You're safe with me, Jennifer," he muttered,

pressing his lips to her temple. "I'd never hurt a woman, especially you." His arms tightened as he swept her into a series of fast, graceful turns.

"I believe you," she replied softly once she was back in his embrace. "At least, not physically. But you're a very attractive man, Chance, and a woman could lose her heart to you."

"Could she?" he rasped, his voice deeper.

"Yes." She nodded, her hair brushing the underside of his chin and his throat. "I don't want a broken heart, Chance."

"I won't break your heart. Come home with me, Jennifer." His fingers trailed over her cheek, tucked a tendril of soft hair behind her ear, and returned to brush over her lower lip. "I've wanted you since the first time I saw you."

"I don't sleep around," she told him honestly. They'd stopped dancing but still stood within the circle of each other's arms. Beyond the balustrade, the lights of the city glowed while on the street below, the faint sounds of traffic drifted upward. Down the length of the stone veranda they'd traversed, a series of French doors were thrown open to the ballroom. Gold light poured out, illuminating the guests at the other end of the veranda as some strolled or leaned on the wide, chest-high stone bulwark and some danced, swaying in time to the orchestra's lush notes. Chance and Jennifer were alone at their end of the long veranda, shadowed except for the spill of soft light that fell through the glass panes of the French doors beside them, drawn closed against the crowded ballroom inside. The yellow light highlighted his face and she searched his features. "In fact...I haven't been with a man since my divorce, and that was more than five years ago."

His eyes darkened, his mouth a sensual curve. "Honey, that's a damned shame. A woman as beautiful as you should be loved often and well." He bent and brushed his mouth over hers, then lingered to slowly trace her lower lip with the tip of his tongue. "Come home with me. Please."

He urged her closer until she rested against his chest, her thighs aligned with his. Jennifer shuddered at the press of her breasts against hard muscles.

"I don't want to complicate my life," she managed to get out. She struggled to remember why she needed to resist him, closing her eyes against the heat that bloomed beneath his lips as he traced the arch of her throat. "Or yours," she added.

"This doesn't have to be complicated," he murmured, his lips on her throat, just below her ear. "It can be whatever we want it to be."

An enticing shiver ran down her spine, and Jenny knew she couldn't resist him. "Just tonight," she whispered. She forced her eyes open and leaned back, cupping his jaw in her palm to tilt his head up. Beard stubble rasped faintly against the sensitive pads of her fingertips, his eyes ablaze with need. "No complications—and after tonight, we go back to waitress and customer. Can we do that?"

She read the objection that flared in his eyes and saw the swift refusal on his face as his jaw flexed and muscles tightened beneath her hand.

"Please," she said softly, desperate to hold on to some shred of control. "I can't make promises beyond tonight."

His fingers tightened on her waist and then he nodded. "All right. If tonight's all you can give me—" he brushed a kiss against her cheek "—I'll take what I can get."

His mouth covered hers with searing heat. Her senses were fogged and she was reeling with want when he lifted his head. He tucked her along his side and led her to an exit. After waiting—for what felt like an eternity—for the valet to bring his car, they were off. Threading her fingers through his to keep her close, he laid her hand palm down on his thigh and covered it with his own as they sped through

Boston traffic, his touch anchoring her to him. Desire seethed, swirling and heating the air between them in the close confines of the car.

Jennifer was only peripherally aware of the neighborhoods they drove through, her senses focused on the man beside her. When he tapped a control on the dash and then turned off the street and beneath a still-rising garage door, she caught a brief glimpse of the exterior of a brick town house before they pulled in.

Chance switched off the engine, the sudden silence enfolding them. His gaze met hers, heat blazing. "If I touch you before we're inside, we won't make it out of the garage."

She swallowed, throat dry. "Okay."

He smiled, the sudden amusement easing the tension. "Unless you have a fantasy about making love in the backseat of a Jag."

She blinked, distracted by the curve of his mouth. "Um, no."

"Too bad," he said, his voice suddenly lower, huskier. "The idea has possibilities. But I don't want our first time to happen in this car, either, so let's go."

Chapter Three

Chance took Jennifer's hand and led her up the stairs, then down the hall to his bedroom.

The clatter of nails on the polished oak floors below was followed by a loud bark.

"That's Butch," Chance reassured her.

Jennifer's eyes widened at the size of the dog racing down the hallway toward them. The black and tan rottweiler skidded to a stop and sat, panting up at Chance with what looked like an ear-to-ear grin.

"I think he's glad you're home," she said, unconsciously inching behind Chance.

"I think you're right." He tugged her forward and into the bedroom. "I'm going to put him in the kitchen with food and water. I'll be right back." He bent, his mouth taking hers with heated possession. Then he disappeared into the hall, the big dog by his side, tail wagging.

Her legs unsteady, Jennifer sat on the edge of the bed, drawing a deep breath into oxygen-starved lungs. She'd barely gotten her bearings when Chance returned. He strode across the room and caught her hands, drawing her to her feet and into his arms. Her wrap slid to the floor in a pool of red silk at her feet, her small evening bag joining it.

Chance cupped her face in his hands, his gaze intent.

"I can't tell you how many times I've thought about you being here—in my room. And in my bed."

He brushed kisses over her jawline, cheeks, temples. Jennifer's eyes drifted closed and his lips moved softly over her lashes and against her sensitive skin. Just that quickly, she fell back into the haze of need and desire so abruptly interrupted moments before.

She threaded her fingers into the thick, silky dark hair at the nape of his neck and urged him closer until his lips met hers.

Heat built, quickly becoming a firestorm as the kiss turned urgent. Without taking his mouth from hers, Chance lowered the zipper at the skirt of her dress. The backless gown had a sewn-in bra and his fingers stroked over the bare skin of her back.

Jennifer reluctantly lowered her arms from around his neck, a quick shrug sending the loosened gown free to pool at her feet. She knew a moment of self-consciousness when Chance stepped back, his dark eyes searing as he swept her from head to toe with one swift glance. She wore only a tiny pair of red lace bikini panties, thigh-high sheer hose and the red stiletto heels.

"Damn, you're beautiful," he murmured, bending to brush a quick, hard kiss against her mouth before taking a step back again.

His gaze focused on hers, he stripped his tie loose and dropped it on the floor, shrugged out of his tux jacket and tossed it behind him.

He caught her waist in his hands and drew her nearer.

"Unbutton my shirt," he instructed, his voice husky with arousal. His thumbs moved in slow circles, as if he was unable to stop caressing her.

Reassured, Jennifer took only seconds to slip the black studs free. When she finished, Chance took them from her cupped hand and dropped them on the nightstand before holding up his hand. Jennifer unfastened the cuff links, one by one, and dropped them on the pile of studs. Chance immediately shrugged out of the shirt, pulling her flush against him, his hands threading into her hair to tilt her face up to his. When his mouth settled over hers, Jennifer sank into the sensation of his soft lips, gentle and demanding all at once.

The hard muscles of his bare chest teased her sensitive breasts, the fabric of his tux slacks faintly rough against her thighs. And his lips on hers sent desire throbbing through her veins.

She murmured incoherently and Chance laid her back on the bed before he stood, toeing off his shoes, pulling off his socks, unzipping and shoving his pants and boxer shorts down his legs. He bent and pulled open the drawer in the bedside table, ripped open a packet and a second later, rolled on protection. Then he leaned over her, slipping his thumbs under the narrow bands of red lace on her hips to tug her panties down her legs. He dropped the bit of lace and silk on the floor behind him before bending to press a kiss against the faint outward curve of her belly.

Jennifer gasped at the heated brush of his mouth against her sensitive skin. He stroked his tongue over the indentation of her belly button and she moaned. Frantic to have him closer, she tugged at his arms, fingers clutching the hard muscles of his biceps to urge him nearer.

He surged on top of her, his mouth taking hers with urgency, one knee nudging hers apart to make space for him. Then he was inside her. Jennifer cried out, drowning in pleasure and need.

It had been too long for her and, all too soon, Chance drove her over the edge.

Sated and drowsy, she opened her eyes and found him gazing at her, a slow smile curved the sensual line of his mouth.

"I'm guessing it was good." His words weren't a question but she nodded, too satisfied and boneless to speak, nonetheless.

"Let's try it again," he murmured against her mouth.

And a moment later, despite being certain she couldn't move a muscle, Jennifer was again burning with heat, twisting urgently beneath his mouth, hands and the steady thrust of his powerful body.

Just after midnight, hunger lured them out of bed and downstairs to raid the refrigerator. Dressed only in Chance's white tux shirt, the long tails hitting her at mid-thigh and sleeves rolled to her elbows, Jennifer perched on a tall stool and propped her elbow on the island countertop, leaning her chin on her hand. The kitchen was beautifully appointed and everywhere she looked, something drew her eye. But after a quick glance around the room, her gaze returned with fascination to Chance. Grey boxer shorts hung low on his hips as he bent to peer into the refrigerator. His powerful shoulders and chest were bare as were his thighs and long legs. Despite the long hours they'd just spent in the bedroom upstairs and although she'd felt sated and content only moments earlier, heat stirred in her belly once again. She shivered as she contemplated running her palms over his back while his weight pinned her to the bed.

"How do you feel about spaghetti and cheesecake?"

Her eyes widened and she straightened. "Yum. What kind of cheesecake?"

He turned to look at her over his shoulder. "Regular, I guess, except it has chocolate on the top."

"Even better," she said promptly.

He grinned at her, eyes warming. "You like chocolate?"

"Of course, who doesn't?" she responded.

"I definitely do. The local café has chocolate crepes so good they can make a grown man cry. We'll get you some for brunch tomorrow." He turned back to the refrigerator and moments later, nudged the door closed with his hip because his hands were full of food containers.

"Here, let me help." She jumped down from the counter and hurried to take a plate of cheesecake from him. He'd balanced it on top of a deep blue casserole dish, where it tilted and wobbled precariously.

"Thanks." Chance slid the casserole onto the tiled counter and removed the glass lid. He stirred the red sauce and spaghetti noodles and popped the dish into the microwave, set the timer and closed the door.

"I think we should seriously consider cutting a bite of cheesecake while we wait for the spaghetti," Jennifer told him, eyeing the swirls of dark chocolate on top of the cake.

"Sure, why not." He took a knife and a fork out of a drawer and joined her, bracketing her against the counter with his arms and body. "You cut." He laid the utensils on the countertop on each side of the cheesecake and bent to nuzzle his face against her nape. His hands settled on her hipbones.

Jennifer closed her eyes, her body going boneless as she melted back against him. His hands slipped beneath the hem of the white shirt and stroked upward, over her belly and midriff to cup her breasts.

"Ohhhh, that's not fair," she moaned as her nipples pebbled against his fingers and her hips settled into the cove of his. She tilted her head back against his shoulder, the thick silk of his hair brushing her throat as he bent over her to press his mouth against the upper curve of her breast.

She twisted in his hold, slipping her arms around his neck, her body pressed flush against his as she tugged his mouth down to hers. His hands cupped her bottom, lifting her higher, and the kiss turned hotter, more carnal.

Behind them, the microwave alarm buzzed loudly as the timer went off.

Chance eased back from the kiss and lifted his head.

"Want to skip the spaghetti and cheesecake and make love on the countertop?" he asked, his voice rasping with need.

Jennifer was torn but before she could decide, her stomach growled. They both laughed.

"That's it. Food wins," he declared, pressing one last hard kiss against her mouth and stepping back. "First we'll feed you, then we'll get naked again. Let's go back to bed."

He reached behind her and picked up the cheese-cake plate, handing it to her with the knife and fork. "You carry this, I'll get the spaghetti."

"What about plates? And don't we need another fork?" she asked, still disoriented and flushed.

"Nope." He used hot pads to remove the casserole of spaghetti and closed the door with his elbow.

"We'll share. But we might need napkins. Grab a couple out of the drawer by your hip, will you?"

Jennifer found snowy-white linen napkins and preceded him down the hall and up the stairs to his bedroom.

Chance tossed the sheet to the bottom of the bed and disappeared into the bathroom, reappearing with a thick blue towel. He spread it on the center of the bed and set the casserole on it.

"We're having a picnic," she said with delight. "I love picnics and I've never had one in bed before."

"The mattress is more comfortable than the floor." Chance crooked his finger at her. "And when we're done eating, the bed's more comfortable for making love."

She laughed, balancing the cheesecake in one hand and utensils in the other as she climbed onto the bed, shuffling on her knees to the far side of the folded towel. "Plus," she told him, setting down the cheesecake, "there are no ants. Always a good thing."

Chance grabbed her free hand and tugged, tumbling her toward him. He threaded his fingers into her hair and kissed her, his mouth hot. "I love the way you find the good in everything. You're easy to please."

"You offered me cheesecake with chocolate." She raised an eyebrow. "Why wouldn't I be pleased?"

"Lots of women would be offended if they weren't offered champagne and caviar."

"Hmm." She eyed him. "I think you've been dating the wrong women."

His eyes laughed at her. "I think you're right."

He stabbed the fork into the spaghetti, twirled it, and lifted the pasta to her mouth. "Tell me if it's hot enough."

Obediently, she parted her lips and took the bite.

"How is it?" he asked.

"Excellent," she told him. "Try it."

They took turns, Chance insisting on feeding her.

When the bowl was empty, Jennifer rolled off the bed and carried the casserole dish to the long oak entertainment center across from the foot of the bed. A flat-screen TV was mounted on a wall bracket and on the polished oak surface below was a stack of books.

"You have a copy of the new Tom Clancy book," she exclaimed. "I didn't even know it was out."

"It's not. I have a friend at the publishing house and he sent me a copy before the release date."

Jennifer tilted the stack of books, reading the titles. "You have mystery, suspense and a couple of nonfiction titles." She picked up one of the books and read the back cover copy. "What other genres do you like? Do you read romantic suspense?"

He frowned. "I don't know. I don't think I've ever read one. Unfortunately, I have to read a lot of medical journals so often my fiction reading has to take second place behind articles."

"I know what you mean. Textbooks have to come first with me, too."

"Come here." Chance patted the bed beside him. "We still have cheesecake to eat." Jennifer put down the stack of books and walked back to the bed, tucking the shirttails neatly beneath her as she sat.

"I bet you were a cute little girl," he told her as he cut the cheesecake with the fork.

"What makes you think so?" she teased, opening her mouth to let him feed her.

"Because you sat down as if your mother trained you to tuck in your skirt and sit properly," he told her with a grin.

"It was my grandmother," she said without thinking, after she'd swallowed.

"I bet you were your grandmother's favorite granddaughter," he told her.

She fed him the bite, fascinated by the movement of strong throat muscles as he swallowed. "I was her only granddaughter," she murmured absently, trailing her fingertips down his throat to his shoulder.

"You're an only child, too?" he asked, surprised.

"Yes." She forced a small smile, deciding to confirm what he probably already knew—that her background was light-years away from what had clearly been his privileged home life. "The only child of divorced parents. My mother declared she didn't want any more children. She was far too busy meeting new men and having fun. I heard that my father remarried several times and had more children but I've never met any of my half-siblings." She kept her gaze on the cheesecake, precisely cutting another bite. "I doubt my childhood was anything like yours."

"Hey," he murmured. His hand cupped her chin, tilting her face gently up until her gaze met his. His dark eyes searched hers. "Except for wishing you were happy, it doesn't matter to me what your parents were like or where you spent your childhood, Jennifer. All I care about is that you're here with me now."

Emotion flooded her. She knew there couldn't be a future for them. All her time over the next few years was already committed to work, school and Annie. But for this night, she could forget about tomorrow and responsibilities. And if she felt things with Chance she'd never felt with anyone before, she'd worry about that tomorrow, too.

"All we have is right now," she whispered, lowering the fork to the plate so she could slip her arms around him. "Let's not waste a moment."

His dark eyes turned hot. Without releasing her, he shoved the towel, cheesecake and utensils onto the floor and bore her backward, his mouth taking hers as his weight settled over her.

Jennifer welcomed the instant rise of desire that swept over her, erasing all thought of tomorrow. There was only this moment and the heavy, powerfully muscled body on hers as Chance's fierce passion carried her over the edge once again.

Jennifer was half-awake the following morning when Chance left the bed. He bent over, kissed her, chuckled and with a pat on her bottom covered by the sheet, left her to disappear into the bathroom. She smiled, half opening her eyes and noting the bright sunshine pouring through the open drapes. Then she yawned and rolled over.

It seemed like only a moment before Chance came back into the bedroom, several pieces of clothing tossed over his arm.

"Hey, sleepy woman, wake up! I promised you crepes for breakfast." He tossed the clothes on the end of the bed. "My mother left some things in the guest room the last time she was here," he told her, dropping onto the bed to stretch out beside her. "The slacks might be a little short but they're bound to fit better than a pair of my jeans."

The bed dipped under his weight, rolling Jennifer toward him. He grinned and caught her, tugging the sheet lower until she was bare from her tousled hair to her belly button.

Chance's head bent and he trailed his lips over the upper curve of her breasts. "Mmm," he muttered. "You taste as good as you look."

Jennifer buried her fingers in the silky thickness of his hair, cradling his head to hold him close as her eyelids drifted closed.

"If we're going out, I have to shower and get dressed," she protested drowsily, smiling as he growled in protest. She closed her fingers into fists and tugged his hair, the strands sliding like rough black silk against her fingertips and palms.

Reluctantly, he obeyed her silent demand and lifted his head to look down at her. "We could skip going out and order in—eat Chinese food in bed," he suggested.

"No." She laughed softly. "I'm starving and those chocolate crepes sound wonderful." And she wanted to see a bit more of the pieces of his day-to-day life. The need to know him better, to learn more about the man behind the handsome face and powerful male body, grew stronger with each moment she spent in his company.

"All right," he grumbled good-naturedly, his hands trailing over her midriff as he rolled onto his side, releasing her so she could slide out of bed. "We'll take Butch for a walk and get brunch at the café. Then we'll come back and pick up where we're leaving off. Deal?"

"Deal." She flashed him a sassy grin, caught up the pile of clothing from the foot of the bed and slipped into the bathroom. For a moment, she leaned back against the door, eyes closed, a smile on her lips while she reveled in the sheer happiness bubbling through her veins.

A half hour later, Jennifer had showered, pulled her hair up into a high ponytail, smoothed on the lipstick and mascara she'd tucked into her evening bag the night before, and was dressed. She paused to run a quick, assessing glance over her reflection in the long mirrors bracketing the door.

The pale pink silk slacks fit well except for being a trifle short in the leg, the hem hitting her at her anklebone. *Which is actually a good thing,* she thought, since if the designer label slacks had been longer, she would have surely tripped over them while wearing the strappy red heels. The white silk tank top was snug and since she didn't have a bra to wear, she'd pulled on a clean white shirt from Chance's closet. It was much too big, of course, but after rolling the sleeves to her elbow, she decided it worked well enough to conceal her braless state.

In fact, she thought, turning to look over her shoulder at her back view, the outfit was rather chic. The slim-cut slacks hugged her thighs below the hem of the loose white shirt, and the red heels added a touch of Vogue-model fashion to the outfit.

Thanks to Chance's mother leaving clothes in his guestroom, Jennifer reflected, she was reasonably covered. She'd had a few qualms about the clothing, suspecting it might have really belonged to one of Chance's girlfriends. But the silk slacks and tank top had a small label with "A. Demetrios" beautifully embroidered in blue and gold thread. Chance had mentioned his parents, John and Anastasia, and Jennifer was confident the "A. Demetrios" was surely his mother.

She left the bathroom, a spring to her step, and went searching for Chance. She found him in the kitchen, reading a newspaper spread out over the island countertop.

"Hey." He looked up when she entered, his eyes lighting up as he swept her from head to toe and back again.

"Hi." Suddenly self-conscious under his intent

stare, she glanced down. "I'm glad your mother left her slacks and top here. Are you sure she won't mind my borrowing them?"

"I'm positive," he told her, abandoning the paper on the counter. He reached her in two long strides and wrapped her close, pressing a quick, hard kiss against her mouth. When he lifted his lips from hers, his eyes were molten. "And if we don't leave the house right now, I'm going to carry you back upstairs. Come on. Let's feed you. You're going to need energy when we get home."

He released her, threaded her fingers through his, and tugged her after him toward the front door.

"Come on, Butch."

The big dog obeyed Chance's command with enthusiasm, pushing past them to race down the hall and wait just inside the front door.

Chance took a leash from a peg on the antique coatrack and clipped it onto Butch's collar, then pulled open the heavy oak door.

Jennifer stepped outside, relishing the balmy air and the quick warmth of sunlight on her bare forearms.

Chance locked the door behind them, pocketing the keys before catching Jennifer's hand in his, and with Butch leading the way at the end of the leash, they set off down the street.

"I love your neighborhood," Jennifer told him, taking in the neat facades of town houses and bright flowers filling window boxes. She tilted her face up and spring sunshine warmed her cheeks, filtered through tree leaves.

"Good morning."

The friendly greeting drew Jennifer's attention and she smiled hello at the young couple passing by, pushing a stroller with a little boy that babbled excitedly, hands outstretched to Butch.

"Good morning." Chance nodded at the couple, letting the little boy pat Butch on the nose, then pulling the big dog away before he could lick the toddler's face.

"Who was that?" Jennifer asked, curious.

"The Carmichaels." Chance expertly steered Butch around a trio of giggling schoolgirls in jeans and sandals walking toward them, three abreast on the sidewalk. "They moved into the house two doors down from me just before their little boy was born. I met them when I was out walking Butch."

"Butch seems to be a great ice breaker," Jennifer commented. "You must meet a lot of people when they stop to pet him."

"Yeah, I do." He grinned at her and tugged her nearer, releasing her hand to sling an arm over her shoulder and tuck her close. Their hips bumped companionably as they walked. "Nobody can resist a big, friendly dog."

Jennifer privately thought it was probably the combination of Butch's friendliness and Chance's charm.

"Here we are." Chance drew Jennifer to a halt outside a small restaurant. "Do you mind sitting outside? I can't take Butch inside."

He nodded at the area to their right. Several round wrought-iron tables with colorful red and white umbrellas shading their chairs were clustered along the front of the café, the uneven line two tables deep. Just then a patron exited, the café's open door releasing a waft of aroma that was mouthwatering.

"Yes, let's." Jennifer drew in a deep breath. "It smells fabulous. I can't believe anyone has the willpower to walk by and not stop to eat."

Chance bent to brush his lips against her ear. "The food's great but it doesn't taste as good as you."

Jennifer shivered with awareness and felt her skin warm.

His arm tightened in a brief hug before he released her and pulled out a chair at an empty table at one end of the row.

He knotted Butch's leash around the arm of a chair. "Stay," he told him as he dropped into the seat.

Butch obligingly lay down between Chance and Jennifer, technically outside the dining area. Ears perked, eyes alight with interest, he watched the diners at the neighboring tables.

The cute young waitress who took their order clearly adored Chance.

"You have another admirer," Jennifer teased as the teenager disappeared into the restaurant.

"Carrie?" he asked. When Jennifer nodded, he grinned at her. "Nah, I'm helping her brother study for his SATs, that's all. He's a bright kid but the family doesn't have the money to send him to a top-notch med school. If he scores high on the SAT, he'll have a better shot at scholarships."

"What a lovely thing for you to do," she told him. "You're a surprise, Dr. Demetrios."

"Why?" he asked, resting his forearms on the tabletop and leaning forward, his gaze searching hers.

"Because you have a reputation as a playboy, which infers you're shallow. But the more I get to know you, the more complicated you seem."

He smiled, a slow upward curve of his lips. "I'm not complicated," he murmured, his voice husky with need. "At the moment, I've got only a single interest."

"And what would that be?" she asked, mesmerized by the heat in his eyes and the sensual curve of his mouth.

"You." He closed the few inches between them and covered her mouth with his.

The kiss was sweet, slow and filled with heat. Jennifer felt her toes curl as desire moved like languid fire through he veins.

"Um, excuse me." The hesitant female voice had Chance lifting his head.

"Ah, coffee." He sat back to give the waitress room to empty her tray, setting steaming coffee cups in front of them and a carafe in the center of the table. "Thanks."

The fresh-faced teenager smiled shyly in response and whisked away.

Jennifer was disoriented and slightly dizzy from the kiss, while Chance appeared to have gone from arousal to casual friendliness in a matter of seconds.

Determined to match his seemingly unflappable coolness, she sipped her coffee, eyeing him over the rim while she scrambled for casual conversation.

"Did you grow up here in Boston?" she asked, settling for a standard, getting-to-know-you topic.

"No." He shook his head. "I spent my childhood in upstate New York. I moved here when I took the job at the Armstrong Institute. What about you—did you grow up in Boston?"

"No, I lived in a small town in Illinois until I moved here last year."

"What made you choose Boston?"

"I had a friend from high school who moved here. She encouraged me to join her. She loved the city, especially all the American historical sites. We used to visit a national historical treasure nearly every weekend."

"Used to? Why did you stop?"

Jennifer shrugged. "Renee met the man of her dreams and it was love at first sight. They married after dating for three weeks and have been traveling the world ever since. He's an archeologist and they're currently living in Central America while he helps excavate a Mayan temple."

"No kidding?" Chance looked intrigued. "Now there's a job that sounds interesting."

Jennifer laughed. "Every guy who hears about Renee's husband's job says that. There must be a frustrated adventurer hidden in every male on the planet."

"Maybe." He grinned.

The waitress arrived with their food, interrupting their conversation. Jennifer indulged in crepes drizzled with chocolate sauce while Chance tucked into a Spanish omelet. By the time they'd finished eating and had poured a second round of coffee, they were deep in a discussion of movies they'd seen.

"You like chick flicks," Chance told her. "Most of the movies on your best-of list are romantic comedies."

"I liked the movie *Hunt For Red October* and that's not a chick flick," Jennifer protested.

"No kidding—you like that movie?" He lifted his brows in surprise. "I've seen it about a dozen times."

"Me, too." Jennifer sipped her coffee. "Of course," she added, "the film's stars are Sean Connery and a young Alec Baldwin. To be honest, I'd be tempted to watch it over again just to see them."

"So the big attraction isn't the incredible underwater sub maneuvers or the great suspense plot, it's the handsome actors?"

She considered the question, eyes narrowed, before nodding firmly. "Pretty much."

Chance's face lit with amusement, his deep, rich laughter drawing the attention of nearby diners.

Jennifer suspected her smile was besotted but she couldn't help it. The sunlight gleamed in his black hair, laugh lines fanning at the corners of his eyes.

His gaze met his and his laughter died.

"Let's go home," he said roughly, the curve of his mouth sensual.

"Yes," she breathed, caught up in the heat that flared between them. "Let's."

Jennifer woke slowly, stretching and smiling contentedly at the warmth against her back. A weight lay over her waist, anchoring her to the hard male body she lay tucked against and she realized Chance was curled around her, his arm holding her close.

There was a great deal to like about waking up with a man, she thought with a smile.

She opened her eyes. Just beyond the edge of the white sheet-covered mattress was the oak night-stand with a brass clock, its numbers glowing in the dim bedroom.

Her eyes widened. It was almost four o'clock. And Linda had promised to return Annie to the apartment by 6:00 p.m.

Her weekend was over.

She wasn't ready to let it go. She'd lost track of the number of times they'd made love and yet she wanted more. But reality intruded and she bit her lip, knowing she had no choice.

Carefully, she lifted Chance's arm and slipped out from beneath his hold. He muttered, protesting, and she froze beside the bed, holding her breath and hoping he wouldn't waken. Then he shifted, sprawling on his stomach over the place where she'd lain moments before. His eyes remained closed and the tension eased out of his big body as he relaxed, clearly asleep again.

Jennifer lingered a moment, her gaze tracing the beard-shadowed line of his jaw, the black lashes fanning against his olive skin and the sensual curve of his mouth. The white sheet was bunched at his waist, leaving the powerful muscles of his upper body and arms bare.

Reluctant to leave him, she forced herself to turn her back and pad silently into the bathroom where she'd left her borrowed clothes earlier. Dressing quickly, she slipped through the connecting door to the hall and let herself out the front door of Chance's town house.

As she hurried down the street on her way to the bus stop on the next block, she was assailed by a barrage of memories of the hours spent with Chance.

He was a man she could easily fall in love with, she realized. She hoped fervently that she hadn't already done so—because she knew there wasn't, could never be, a future for them together. She reached the end of the block and a bus wheezed to a stop, the doors opening. She climbed the steps, determined to put Chance Demetrios out of her mind.

Whether she could put him out of her heart remained to be seen.

Chance knew the moment he woke that Jennifer was gone. He swept his hand over the sheet but felt no warmth left by her body. He sat up, scrubbing his hands over his face, then tilted his head, listening. The complete silence was broken only by the soft ticking of the bedside clock.

"Damn it," he said into the stillness. He'd wanted to take her home. He hadn't counted on being so relaxed and wrung out from making love this morning and last night that he'd sleep through Jennifer's leaving.

Nails clattered on the oak flooring and Butch nosed the hall door open wider before bounding across the room, tail wagging. He laid his head on the bed, big brown eyes pleading with Chance.

"What?" Chance groaned. "I suppose you want to go out?"

The big rottweiler barked, one sharp, approving sound that made Chance wince.

"Not so loud, buddy," he muttered. "I'm getting up."

He tossed back the sheet and sat on the edge of the bed.

Butch barked again and nosed the sheet a few inches

from Chance's hip, burrowing beneath the sheet until his head was out of sight beneath white cotton.

"Hey, cut that out." Chance tossed the sheet aside. Silver glittered and he pulled the sheet aside to find a necklace peeking out from under the pillow. He grabbed the chain and locket just before Butch could reach it. A low whine rumbled from the dog's throat and his brown eyes were reproachful. "Oh, come on." Chance ran his hand over Butch's head and scratched him behind his ear. "You know this is Jennifer's. And you know you're not supposed to have it."

Butch plopped down on his haunches and eyed the locket, dangling by its chain from Chance's fingers.

The oval-shaped locket had a delicate latch. Chance felt as if his fingers were giant-size as he carefully maneuvered the tiny mechanism. The locket opened and he held it on his palm. One side held a photograph of a little girl, her impish face smiling up at him. The other half held a tiny curl of auburn hair, gleaming brightly against the silver metal.

Cute kid. I wonder who she is? He ran the pad of his index finger over the small, bright curl. *And I wonder if this is her hair?*

He had no answers, but he was going to ask Jennifer as soon as he saw her again. There were lots of things he wanted to know about her. Their one date—

and the best sex he'd ever shared—had only led him to be more intrigued about her.

Butch whined and nudged his damp nose against Chance's knee.

"Okay, big guy," Chance told him. "I'll let you out."

He grabbed his jeans from the closet and pulled them on. Then he jogged barefoot down the stairs and through the kitchen to open the back door. Butch barreled happily past him and out into the small backyard.

"I've got to teach him better manners," Chance muttered to himself. He turned back into the kitchen to make coffee—and wondered if Jennifer was thinking of him, as he was thinking of her.

Jennifer stepped out of the silk slacks and folded them atop the hamper. She knew by the label that the slacks had probably cost more than her monthly salary, the nubby raw silk pure tactile pleasure to touch.

I'll drop them at the cleaners after work tomorrow, she thought. *Along with the top. Then I'll mail them back to Chance.*

She pulled the tank off over her head, folding it neatly atop the slacks, before she turned on the sink taps. Cupping her hands, she splashed cool water on her face, reaching blindly for a hand towel. She blotted moisture from her skin before tugging the band from her ponytail. As it pulled free and let her hair tumble about her shoulders, she ran her fingertip over the base of her throat. The gesture was pure habit. She'd worn the locket with Annie's picture and lock of hair since her daughter was born.

But this time…the chain wasn't there.

Dismayed, Jennifer stared with consternation at her reflection in the mirror. She knew she'd been wearing it earlier in the day when she'd dressed to go out to brunch. Frowning, she mentally reviewed the afternoon and realized that the last time she'd noticed the locket was after they'd returned to the town house. Chance had rushed her upstairs and stripped off their clothes before tossing her on the bed. He'd joined her immediately and she remembered the slide of cool metal over her skin when Chance's lips brushed the locket aside, replacing it with his mouth.

Maybe I lost it in his bed, she thought. She hoped the locket had ended up tangled in Chance's sheets rather than broken and lost on the street or the bus.

She would have to call Chance and ask if he'd found her missing locket. Misgiving warred with delight at the thought. She wasn't sure she had the fortitude to walk away from him a second time.

The night with Chance was a fairy tale—a few days stolen for herself, Jennifer thought later that evening.

With Annie tucked into bed after telling Jennifer about the fun things she did with Linda's children, Jennifer walked back into the living room and dropped onto the sofa.

She switched on the television, browsing through channels with the remote control and finally settling on a news station. Dressed in pajama bottoms and a white cotton camisole, she tucked her legs under her and stared blindly at the TV screen. She couldn't make herself care about the political news or the latest scandal caused by a local state representative.

She couldn't stop thinking about Chance.

It wasn't just the sex—which had been amazing. It was his sense of humor, the discovery that they both loved or disliked some of the same movies. They'd argued hotly in defense of book titles the other had merely shrugged over but, each time, the contention had ended with laughter and kisses.

She'd never met anyone like Chance before.

And now that her night with him was over, she had to admit that spending time with him meant more to her than a brief, spicy interlude to her nonexistent dating life.

She had feelings for him. She wasn't sure exactly what those feelings were, or how deeply they ran, but the ache in her heart wasn't simple. That nothing could ever grow between them only made her chest hurt more.

There was no possible future between a waitress at the Coach House Diner and a doctor at the Armstrong Fertility Institute. Their lives were too different; the disparity in their background and income too great. She wouldn't see him anymore, outside the diner.

Jennifer knew it was for the best but somehow the thought of going back to pouring Chance his morning coffee while knowing she'd never be more than a one-time date made her pain grow.

It's no good yearning for the moon, she told herself stoutly, wiping dampness from her cheeks. *I knew when I agreed to go out with him that it was a one-shot deal. No future dates, no building dreams of a relationship.*

She switched off the television and the living-room lights, entering her bedroom where the bedside lamp threw a pool of soft white over her solitary bed.

It's time for Cinderella to go back to her real life, she told herself as she climbed into bed and switched off the lamp. The room was plunged into darkness except for the faint glimmers from the streetlights outside marking the edges of the window blinds.

Resolutely, she closed her eyes but when at last she slept, she dreamed of Chance.

Chance had barely shrugged into his lab coat on Monday when the phone on his desk rang. The caller was Paul Armstrong's secretary, who relayed a message that he was needed in Paul's office immediately.

Wondering what could possibly have happened to impact his research funding this time, he left his office and headed down the hall.

He tapped on the half-open door to Paul's office and stepped inside. "Morning, Paul…Ramona."

"Good morning, Chance." Paul leaned against the front of his desk, hands tucked into his slacks pockets. Ramona Tate, the institute's blonde, blue-eyed public relations expert—and Paul's fiancée—smiled warmly.

Chance didn't miss the worry on both their faces, however, and he mentally braced himself. "Is everything all right?"

"I'm afraid not," Paul said grimly. "There's no easy way to tell you this so I'll just say it—a former patient has filed a paternity suit and named you as the father of her baby."

Chance was stunned. Of all the possible subjects for bad news, this one had never occurred to him.

"That's crazy," he said when he could speak. "Totally insane. Who filed the suit?"

"Georgina Appleby."

Chance bit off a curse.

"I know." Paul grimaced, shifting to cross his arms across his chest. "The institute is behind you one hundred percent in this, Chance. Whatever we can do to help, we will. Just let us know."

"I'm so sorry," Ramona said with sympathy. "The timing of this lawsuit is just terrible. You've barely had time to relax after proving how false those outrageous allegations were about funding for your research with Ted."

"I have no doubt you'll win the day in this, too," Paul told him resolutely.

"Thanks." Chance frowned and raked one hand through his hair, thinking out loud. "I should call my attorney. Has the institute been officially served with copies of the documents?"

"Yes. I had my secretary run a copy for you." Paul picked up a sheaf of papers and handed them to Chance. He turned back to his desk and picked up a copy of the *Boston Herald,* passing that over, as well. "The newspapers already have the details."

Chance took the paper, folded open to the society page. Heavy black marker circled two paragraphs of the gossip column with quotes from Georgina Appleby. "She stops just short of slander," he said grimly.

"No one who knows you will believe it," Ramona stated firmly.

"Maybe," Chance commented, rereading the last paragraph, coldly furious. "I'd like to take this to my attorney, as well."

"Keep it," Paul told him. "I read it on the way to work this morning."

"I'd also like to take a short leave of absence to deal with this," Chance suggested. "The smear against my reputation is probably unavoidable, at least temporarily, but I don't want to damage the institute's image with bad personal publicity."

"Take as much time as you need," Paul said.

"Thanks. My hope is that my attorney can expedite arrangements for an HLA paternity test. Once the results are back, I can prove the case has no merit and I can come back to work. Without being followed by reporters and bad press," he added, shaking his head.

"Sounds good," Paul replied.

"I didn't get to see much of you at the Founder's Ball," Chance noted in a purposely abrupt change of subject.

"We saw you with a stunningly lovely blonde

woman," Ramona commented, following his lead. "But you left before we had a chance to learn who she was."

"I'm keeping her identity a secret," Chance told her with a faint grin.

"Oh, yeah?" Paul lifted an eyebrow, the look he gave Chance speculative.

"Yeah." Chance didn't respond further, guessing that Paul had picked up on the possessive note in his voice. "How's your mother, Ramona?"

Ramona brightened, exchanging a quick glance with Paul. "My half sister, Victoria, has agreed to donate bone marrow so I'm very hopeful that her prognosis will improve."

"I'm glad to hear that," Chance told her. "Very glad."

"Dr. Armstrong?" Paul's secretary tapped on the door panel, then peered into the room. "I'm so sorry to intrude, but Senator Johnson is on the line. He wants to talk to you about a potential donation from a constituent."

"I'm sorry, Chance. I have to take this call." Paul pushed away from the desk.

"Of course. I'll let you know about any developments." Chance headed for the door.

"Take care," Ramona called after him. "Remember, we're here if there's anything we can do to help."

"I appreciate that." Chance lifted a hand in reply

and left the office, striding down the hallway and back to his own office.

He shrugged out of his lab coat and pulled on his leather jacket. Within seconds, he left the office with the sheaf of lawsuit papers in his hand. His partner, Ted, was at his desk and apparently deeply immersed in a report when Chance paused in the doorway.

"Hey, Ted." He waited until Ted looked up. "I'll be out of the office for a few days but if anything comes up, you can reach me on my cell phone."

Ted blinked in surprise, frowning. "What's up? You okay?"

"I'm fine." Chance lifted the lawsuit documents. Ted's gaze flicked to the papers and he frowned as he looked back at Chance. Before he could ask, Chance interrupted him. "Long story. I'll explain later."

"All right."

Chance nodded and turned to leave, stopping when Ted called after him. "Hey, if you need me, call."

Chance glanced over his shoulder and grinned. "I will. A guy never knows when he might need help disposing of a body. I'll keep you on speed dial."

Ted snorted and Chance strode off down the hall.

It was good to know he had friends who would stand by him if he needed help.

Not that he'd need help with this, he thought with

a dismissive frown. Georgina Appleby was a young woman with emotional problems. Even if he'd wanted to compromise his professional principles to sleep with her, her emotional vulnerability would have stopped him.

He'd been concerned about her stability when she'd originally come to him for help with fertility issues. His doubts had deepened when her actions became erratic. He'd referred her to a fellow physician who specialized in patients with her particular combination of conception problems and emotional issues.

Though he'd known she was emotionally unstable, it hadn't occurred to him to consider whether she was mentally unbalanced.

Which is what she must be to file a paternity suit when a blood test will easily prove I'm not the father of her child, he thought grimly. He could only imagine the kind of lawyer who would agree to take such a frivolous case.

He dialed his attorney's office while walking to his car and having confirmed a meeting within a half hour, drove away from the institute. The route to his attorney's office took him down the street, past the Coach House Diner.

Damn it, he thought with frustration. He didn't want to spend the day fighting another unfounded allegation against his good name. He'd been scheduled to run a test analysis in the research lab today. Then he'd planned to order a dozen roses and knock on Jennifer's door to deliver them in person. The night she'd spent in his bed had rocked his world and he was uncharacteristically unsure of her. He felt driven to cement their connection as soon as possible.

He smacked the heel of his hand against the leather-covered steering wheel in frustration. He had to get rid of the paternity suit and return to his normal life—and Jennifer.

The meeting with his attorney went well. He advised Chance to go home and search through his patient files to identify all contact with Georgina Appleby. The attorney wanted details of each time she'd had an appointment with Chance.

He had also been adamant that Chance maintain a low profile—and specifically told him not to date anyone, warning him that he was likely to be followed by reporters in search of fuel for the gossip columns.

Their conversation convinced Chance that he needed to protect Jennifer from unwanted publicity—which meant that just as he would stay away from the Armstrong Fertility Institute offices, he also had to stay away from the diner.

Fortunately, an appointment for the HLA blood

test was set within the week and once the results were back, Chance knew he'd be cleared—and free to see Jennifer again.

Still, putting his plans on hold, though necessary to protect her, didn't sit well.

He dialed her home number from his cell phone but reached her answering machine. Finally, unwilling to explain the situation without speaking to her in person, he left a brief explanation telling her that something important had come up and he would be in touch in about a week.

Edgy and restless, frustrated that he hadn't been able to talk to Jennifer in person, he drove home. His neighborhood was bursting with spring color—pale green leaves unfurling on trees and window boxes blooming with brilliant purple, blue, yellow and pink flowers. Although he'd chosen to buy his town house in part because of the charming neighborhood, today Chance barely noticed his surroundings. He was preoccupied with how much he'd wanted to talk to Jennifer in person. If he couldn't see her, he needed to hear her voice.

He tossed his car keys on the kitchen's tiled island countertop and switched on the coffeemaker. Within moments, the aroma of brewing coffee filled the air. Just as the timer beeped to announce the coffee was ready to pour, the door knocker sounded, its rapping echoing through the entryway and into the kitchen.

Chance strode down the hallway and pulled open the door. A distinguished, silver-haired man in a gray suit stood on the porch, a chauffeur-driven, long black town car parked at the curb behind him.

"Hi, Dad." Chance stepped back, holding the door wide. "This is a surprise—I didn't know you were in town."

"I have a dinner meeting with a group of investors tonight." Jonathon Demetrios walked past his son and into the oak-floored entryway. "Since I have a free hour, I thought I'd drop by to say hello."

Not bloody likely, Chance thought, wondering what had really brought his father to Boston. Whatever it was, he knew from past experience that it was easier to let John Demetrios have his say, then usher him out the door as quickly as possible.

"Come into the kitchen," he said aloud. "I just made a fresh pot of coffee."

When his father was seated on one of the chrome and black suede stools, a mug of coffee on the counter in front of him, Chance picked up his own steaming mug.

"Why don't you tell me why you're really here,

Dad," he said, leaning his hips against the cabinet counter behind him.

"All right." John took a newspaper clipping from his inner jacket pocket and slid it across the counter toward Chance. "Your mother and I are concerned about this woman you're dating."

Chance picked up the clipping, his gaze narrowing over the black and white picture. The photographer for the Boston newspaper's society page had captured him dancing with Jennifer. There was no use denying the expression on his face or hers—the photo highlighted the smoldering attraction between them.

"Nice snapshot," he commented.

"That's not the point," John said impatiently, frowning.

"What *is* the point, Dad?"

"The point," John urged with emphasis, "is that this young woman is a waitress at a local diner. Certainly not the kind of person my heir should be escorting to an important social event."

Chance bit off a curse. He didn't bother asking his father how he knew Jennifer was a waitress and where she worked. John Demetrios had a staff of attorneys at his beck and call. He'd probably had an investigator's detailed report about Jennifer on his desk within twenty-four hours of seeing the photo. He scrubbed his hand down his face and eyed his father wearily. "Don't tell me that you're here to deliver the proper-behavior-for-the-Demetrios-heir lecture again, Dad. I thought you realized I won't listen after the last time we did this."

"The last time you dated inappropriate women was your senior year in college," John snapped. "In the intervening years, your mother and I assumed you'd matured and now had better sense. You have obligations, Chance, whether you want to acknowledge them or not."

Chance held up his hand, palm out. "Don't, Dad. Just…don't." He drew a deep breath to keep from raising his voice. "Who I date is my business. And I will never choose a woman based on a set of antiquated rules created by you and Mom. Certainly not based on whether the woman is suitable for a Demetrios heir. And when I marry—*if* I ever marry," he added when his father flushed with anger, his mouth opening to speak, "I'll choose the woman. And it's not likely she'll be someone from the handful of families approved by you and Mom."

"You have an obligation to the family name," John spoke tightly. "For years, your mother and I have been tolerant of your rebelliousness, hoping you'd eventually take your proper place…."

"Father." Chance held on to his temper with an effort. "My proper place is helping my patients. I'm a doctor. I'm never going to live the life of a trust fund baby. I told you and Mother when I entered med school—my first obligation will always be to my patients."

"I suppose this waitress you're dating thinks she's struck gold," John condemned scathingly. "Not only is she dating a doctor, but you're a Demetrios."

Chance considered the older man while he fought to hold on to his temper. "You know," he said slowly, "I doubt she even knows who the Demetrios family is. Or that she would give a damn."

"Humph." John stood, straightening his jacket with annoyed tugs. "That's highly unlikely. Young women in her class always want to move up. She knows who you are, all right."

"I'm going to forget you said that," Chance said evenly. "But in the future, don't make disparaging remarks about Jennifer."

His father's eyes widened, his expression taken aback. "Are you saying you're actually serious about this woman?"

"I'm saying I don't want her harmed because my father is a snob," Chance explained bluntly.

"You may think I'm a snob, but I've had more experience in these matters than you," John told him flatly. "Getting involved with women outside our class invariably leads to disaster. I've seen it happen over and over again with friends and family."

"We'll have to agree to disagree," Chance countered, as unconvinced now as he had been by his parents' arguments on the subject since he was fourteen. "Is Mother looking forward to the cruise you booked for her birthday?"

Fortunately for Chance's temper, his father allowed the change of subject and didn't return to his warnings about dating Jennifer. A half hour later, Chance closed the door on John's departing back.

"I love them but my family makes me crazy," he muttered to himself as he headed down the hall to his home office. And he considered himself damn lucky they didn't seem to know about the paternity suit yet.

But unfortunately for Chance, the picture of him and Jennifer at the ball and the gossip column paragraphs weren't the only items that included the Demetrios name. The following afternoon, he opened the *Boston Herald* and found a quarter-page article with the details of the paternity suit featured prominently in the local news section. The story was accompanied by a grainy photo of Georgina Appleby side-by-side with a photo of him.

He swore out loud and headed for the shower. Dressing in record time, he drove to the diner. Much to his frustration, Jennifer had already completed her shift and gone home.

"Will you tell her I came by?" he asked Linda, the blonde waitress he'd seen often talking with Jennifer.

"Sure." She poured coffee in his mug. "But why don't you just give her a call? Or drop by her apartment?"

Chance didn't want to confess he'd left several messages on Jennifer's answering machine but she hadn't returned his calls. He was beginning to suspect she was having second thoughts about spending the night with him. And if she'd read about the lawsuit, he wouldn't blame her.

"I can't go by her apartment. I'm being followed by a photographer for the *Boston Herald*'s gossip columnist. I recognized him when I parked in front of the clinic," he informed her. "And I don't want the guy following me to Jennifer's house. I'd just as soon keep her off his radar."

Linda's eyes widened. "Is this because you took Jennifer to the Founder's Ball?"

"No." He shook his head. "Something else."

"Is he following you now? Where is he?" she whispered, glancing furtively behind her.

"Sitting in the booth nearest the door."

She twisted, craning her neck to see around an older couple on their way to the exit. "The little guy with the hat? Is that him?" She looked back at Chance and sniffed. "He doesn't look like he's big enough to cause you any trouble."

"Maybe not, but that camera of his makes a powerful weapon," Chance said dejectedly.

The waitress leaned closer. "Would you like us to keep him here while you leave out the back?"

"I appreciate the offer, but he's been parked outside my house so he knows where I live. He'd just go back there and wait for me."

"What on earth did you do that has a reporter following you?" Her eyes were curious.

"Not a damn thing," Chance growled. "But it's going to take a week or so to clear up what he *thinks* I did and in the meantime, I'm stuck with having reporters tailing me."

"Well, keep him away from Jennifer," Linda advised. "I don't think she'd appreciate having a reporter camped on her doorstep. She's a very private person."

That was just what he was afraid of, Chance thought, though he didn't voice his concern about dragging Jennifer into the gossip storm currently harassing his personal life. "I respect that," he said instead. "And I don't want the gossip columnists to know I'm seeing her."

Linda smiled at him with quick warmth. "It's nice to see a guy concerned about her protection."

Something about the way she phrased the statement set off warning bells for Chance. "That sounds as if somebody hasn't protected her in the past…"

Linda grimaced and waved a hand dismissively. "The last guy she was involved with was her husband. I've never met him but he sounds like a jerk," she said bluntly. "If any of Jennifer's friends thought you were anything like him, we'd form a posse and come after you," she warned.

Chance nodded solemnly, acknowledging the not-so-subtle threat. "If I treated her badly, I'd deserve it," he conceded.

"Good to know." She lifted her head, glancing over her shoulder to nod at the cook. "I have to go." She looked back at him. "Are you sure I can't get you something besides coffee?"

"No, thanks."

She leaned closer, her expression serious. "Take care of our girl, Doc. We think a lot of her."

"So do I."

His response seemed to satisfy her and she nodded abruptly before hurrying off.

Chance drained his mug and rose, shoved a hand in his jeans pocket for cash and counted out bills before tossing several on the table. Then he headed for the exit, pausing to allow an elderly woman to hobble past before he left the diner, the doorbell jingling musically.

At the moment Chance walked out of the Coach House Diner in Boston, in New York City, Jonathon Demetrios finished reading the article detailing the paternity action involving his son.

His mouth tight with anger, he closed the door to his office to keep his wife from hearing and dialed a number while walking back to the desk.

"Maxwell Detective Agency."

"I want to speak with Andrew Maxwell."

"One moment, please."

While he waited, Jonathon reread the article, his anger growing.

He knew very well his son would be furious if he ever learned his father had interfered. Nonetheless, the scandal threatened the entire family with damage to their good name.

And while I'm having this Georgina Appleby investigated, I might as well have Andrew look deeper into the background of this waitress, too, Jonathon decided.

"Maxwell here." The deep voice was abrupt, businesslike.

"Andrew—this is Jonathon Demetrios. I want you to investigate two women. I need the information as soon as possible."

Chapter Four

When Jennifer arrived at the diner for her normal shift the following morning, Linda and Yolanda immediately dragged her into a corner.

"The gorgeous doctor was here yesterday, looking for you," Yolanda told her.

"And someone is following him, so he can't come to your house," Linda added. "He said a photographer was trailing him."

"We saw him," Yolanda interjected, her eyes bright.

"Chance? Or the gossip columnist?"

"No, Jennifer—we saw the photographer. And

then, we saw the article." Linda ducked down to take a folded newspaper from beneath the counter. The five seats at the end of the counter where the trio stood were empty and Linda spread open the paper on the countertop.

With a sense of dread, Jennifer slipped onto one of the stools and read the article. The grainy photos weren't very good likenesses but the man was unquestionably Chance—and the information in the article was undeniably damaging. The reporter quoted the woman as saying she was "heartbroken by the betrayal of the man she loved—and whom she believed loved her." She'd gone on to say Chance had "treated her unkindly and abandoned her."

"I don't believe any of this," Jennifer stated with conviction. She tapped her fingertip on the paper. "The man we've observed every morning for months is not the man she's describing." She folded the paper and handed it back to Linda. "I simply don't believe it."

"But, honey," Yolanda pointed out kindly, "nice men accidentally get women pregnant, too—it happens all the time. Okay, so this woman made some harsh accusations about Chance. But if you set those aside, it's still possible that he's the father of her child. He has quite a reputation with the ladies."

Yolanda was right—Jennifer knew she was right and, much to her dismay, the possibility that Chance had been careless and created an unwanted child with another woman sent a shaft of pain through her chest.

He's not mine, she told herself. *And there never was any possibility of a relationship between us, certainly nothing serious.*

So why did it feel as if her heart was breaking?

With painful honesty, Jennifer realized that on some level, she'd been secretly dreaming that Chance would want a future with her. Had fantasized that the two of them would find a way to be together.

Which was ridiculous, of course. The knowledge made her want to cry.

It's a good thing I haven't returned his calls, she decided, making a vow she wouldn't return any in the future either, no matter how many messages he left.

A clean break was surely best.

A week passed before Chance appeared at the diner. Jennifer had her back turned, handing an order slip to the cook, when she heard the strap of bells on the door jingle. She glanced over her shoulder and her heart leaped.

Chance's dark gaze met hers, his eyes warm. An exiting customer walked between them, blocking him and he shifted, smiling at her before he moved down the aisle to reach a booth in her section.

Jennifer passed Yolanda as she walked behind the counter. "Will you tell the boss I'm taking my break now?"

"Sure." Yolanda looked up. "What are you…?" She glanced past Jennifer and saw Chance sliding into the seat of a booth. "Oh."

Chance stood as Jennifer reached the booth, waiting until she took the bench opposite him.

"Hello," she said gravely.

"Hello," he responded, voice husky. "I've left messages on your machine. You didn't call back."

"I didn't think I should," she explained truthfully. "We agreed that our…date…was a one-night thing. And that after it was over, we'd return to our normal lives as if it had never happened."

"That's right, we did." A faint frown veed his brows, his gaze intent on her face. "Is that what you want?"

"I thought it's what you wanted," she commented. "When you didn't come into the diner all week, I was certain of it."

"I couldn't come near you," he told her grimly. "Not without involving you in a scandal."

"You mean the paternity suit?" she asked quietly.

"Yes." He thrust his hand through his hair, raking

it back from his forehead. "I suppose you read about it in the papers?"

"It was hard to miss," she told him.

"Yeah, it was." He frowned, a cynical twist to his mouth. "And of course, the columnist who broke the story didn't bother to comment on the conclusion."

"The conclusion?"

"I called in a few favors and had my blood tests expedited. The results came back today. They prove I'm excluded as a possible father of the child."

Relief flooded through Jennifer and she realized that in some hidden part of her heart, she'd been unsure of his innocence. His words soothed some bruised, wary place inside her. She leaned forward, impulsively covering his hands with hers atop the table. "I'm so glad this was resolved so quickly for you, Chance. Linda and Yolanda told me you were being followed by a photographer. That must have been awful."

"The photographer is the reason I haven't tried to see you." Chance turned his palms upward, capturing her hands in his. "If he'd seen us together, our photo would be splashed all over the papers the next day. That kind of attention isn't comfortable—I wanted to protect you from it."

Touched, Jennifer squeezed his hands. "That was

very sweet of you. And very considerate," she added, thinking about how awful it would have been if Annie had been photographed and their lives laid bare to public gossip.

"No," Chance said, his thumbs moving in slow, rhythmic strokes over the back of her hands. "It should never have happened." He leaned forward, his gaze intent on hers. "The woman who accused me of fathering her child was an ex-patient. I can't discuss details but I want you to know that I never touched her, other than in a purely professional way. I was her doctor for a short time and then referred her to a physician friend who I felt was more qualified to deal with her situation. There was never the slightest moment of inappropriate contact between us. Our relationship was strictly doctor and patient."

"I believe you," Jennifer assured him. His features eased, lines disappearing from around his mouth and eyes, and she realized that he'd been unsure of her reaction. "Chance, I've watched you interact with other customers here in the diner over the past six months. You've been unfailingly kind and considerate to people, whether young or old. And I've never once seen you respond with anything but friendly politeness when women have obviously been coming on to you. Not that I'm unaware of your reputation as a lady-killer," she added with a wry smile. "Goodness knows, the female half of the institute's employees who have lunch here seem to spend fifty percent of their time speculating about your love life."

"I can't help what people say about me," he told her, his eyes serious. "And I admit I like women and that I've dated quite a few over the years. But I would never get a woman pregnant and then abandon her. Kids are too important. I'd never walk away from a child of mine."

Jennifer's heart clenched. Her ex-husband hadn't wanted a baby and by filing for divorce while she was pregnant, he'd effectively abandoned her. That Chance obviously felt strongly about the father standing by the mother of his child sent elation bubbling through her veins.

Perhaps there truly were men in the world with a sense of responsibility, she thought. And who would have expected a well-known playboy to be one of those men?

"It's wonderful to know you wouldn't ignore your responsibility to your child, even if conception was unplanned," she reiterated. Emotion trembled in her voice and she didn't miss his quick frown of concern. Before he could ask her any questions, however, she rushed into speech. "Will the lawsuit be dismissed, now that the test results have excluded you?"

He nodded. "My attorney is working on that now. I suspect my former patient filed the case as leverage to negotiate a settlement. There are no grounds for a payoff now, of course."

"She damaged your reputation and caused all this trouble because she wanted money?" Jennifer's eyes widened, shock giving way to outrage on his behalf.

"I'm sure that was the motive." He shrugged, his mouth curving into a wry smile that didn't reach his eyes.

"Has this happened before?" Jennifer asked, struck by his calmness.

"Not with a paternity suit." His dark gaze was unreadable. "I have a good income from my medical career, Jennifer, but my parents are…fairly well-off, too. Over the years, several people have tried various schemes to extract money from us." He shook his head. "We've never given in."

Appalled, Jennifer couldn't speak for a moment. "Have you ever been hurt?" she asked, horrified images of television reports of kidnappings and robberies flashing in her brain.

"No." He shook his head again. "Never—the

attempts have involved what police might refer to as white-collar crime, always civil law actions."

"That's terrible." She had no experience to compare with this. Jennifer couldn't imagine dealing with criminal or civil greed targeting her.

"Mostly it's just annoying," he told her. "The family has excellent attorneys and I've learned to let them handle these situations." He squeezed her hands. "It does no good to worry over it—and in the meantime," he continued, "life goes on." He leaned back and shoved one hand into his jeans pocket.

"I've wanted to return this to you all week," he told her, holding out his hand. A delicate silver chain dangled from his hand, a silver locket suspended over his palm.

"My locket!" Jennifer exclaimed with pleasure. "Where did you find it?" She took the pretty necklace from his outstretched hand and fastened it around her neck.

"Butch found it." He dropped his voice to a deep murmur. "In my bed."

Her gaze flew to his and she felt her cheeks heat. She couldn't look away, memories swirling as his deep chocolate eyes turned hot.

"I, um…" She faltered, drawing a deep breath.

"I want to see you again, Jennifer."

"You are seeing me," she noted.

"I mean outside the diner. I know we had an agreement," he said. "But one night wasn't enough. If anything, all it did was convince me that we should see each other again."

Jennifer badly wanted to say yes but she was torn. She'd vowed before Annie was born that she wouldn't expose her daughter to a succession of men friends. At least, not until she knew the relationship was serious. And she had no clue whether Chance contemplated a future. Given his history with women, she doubted it.

Not to mention that she had so little free time between her job at the diner, caring for Annie and her college classes.

Still, she'd discovered during the night she'd spent with Chance that he was more complicated, more complex, more loving and certainly more fun than she'd expected.

She wanted to know him better. But how to do that without breaking her commitments to Annie, work and school?

"I have a class tonight that I can't skip," she said slowly. "But I can meet you for coffee afterward, if you'd like?"

"I'd like," he agreed promptly.

They arranged to meet outside the campus library after her class and Chance said goodbye.

"Did he tell you about the paternity suit?" Linda asked when Jennifer relieved her behind the counter.

"Yes, there were blood tests and they proved he's not the father." Jennifer walked the length of the counter, pouring coffee into customers' cups and exchanging hellos with her regulars before returning to the center section where Linda waited. "We're meeting for coffee after my class tonight."

"Yes!" Linda crowed, her smile wide. "That's terrific, Jennifer."

"I'm not sure if it is or isn't, but I know I want to see him again."

"Trust me," Linda said firmly. "You and the doc are great together. Dating him is going to be soooo good for you."

"Who's dating?" Shirley asked as she and Yolanda joined them.

"I'm meeting Chance tonight after my class," Jennifer whispered, aware of the interested customers within hearing range.

"Cool." Shirley's eyes were bright with approval.

"Now you're doing the smart thing," Yolanda told her. "That man is fine." She rolled her eyes and the other three laughed out loud.

"Hey, are you four working or talking?" the boss yelled from the pass-through window into the kitchen.

They exchanged guilty glances and dispersed, Yolanda winking at Jennifer as they left the counter to wait on customers in the booths.

When Jennifer called her neighbor and babysitter, Margaret Sullivan, to tell her that she was meeting someone for coffee after class, Margaret was delighted. She assured Jennifer she was happy to stay later than usual with Annie and told her to enjoy herself.

Since Annie was accustomed to having Margaret stay with her while Jennifer was at class, Jennifer didn't feel too guilty about staying out later than usual. In any event, Annie was always asleep when Jennifer returned and would never know if her mom was out later than usual.

Try as she might, Jennifer had difficulty concentrating on the classroom lecture. Although she took as many pages of notes as usual, her attention wasn't fully concentrated on the speaker. When at last the instructor released the group, she took a moment to slick a fresh coat of color on her lips before leaving the lecture hall.

Chance leaned against a waist-high wall outside the library entryway. His hands tucked into the pockets of faded jeans, he scanned the passing groups of chattering students, looking for Jennifer.

He saw her hair first. Long caramel-blond silk caught up in a ponytail, she walked a few steps behind a quartet of younger students. Lust stirred as he watched her walk toward him, her long legs encased in jeans, a plain white scoop-necked T-shirt tucked in the belted waistband, simple black flats on her narrow feet and a pale blue sweater over her shoulders.

He wanted to take her to bed. Now. But strangely enough, he was willing—hell, he was even happy— to know he'd get to spend innocent time talking with her at a coffee shop.

His stomach growled.

He needed more than coffee, he realized, counting the hours since he'd grabbed a sandwich at lunch.

"Hi, there." She reached him just as he pushed away from the wall.

"Hello, beautiful." He couldn't resist bending to brush a kiss against her cheek, just at the corner of her soft mouth.

Even in the light from streetlamps and the library windows behind them, he could see the color flush her cheeks.

"Are you hungry?" he asked, hooking an arm around her shoulders to anchor her against his side. He took the books from her hands and tucked them under his free arm before urging her into motion. "Because I just realized I missed dinner and I'm starving."

"I had a cup of soup before class but I guess I could have a bite of something." She looked up at him, her ponytail brushing silkily against his cheek as she moved. "Did you have somewhere in mind?"

He nodded. "There's a great Italian restaurant just down the block. How do you feel about pasta?"

"I love pasta," she told him.

"Great."

A half hour later, they were seated across from each other at a table covered with a red-checked cloth. The table was lit with a white candle in a squat wine bottle, its green glass half-covered with drippings of melted wax. Plates of lasagna, green salad and stemmed glasses filled with ruby red wine sat in front of them.

Jennifer took another bite of lasagna and sighed, half closing her eyes as she swallowed. "This lasagna is fabulous," she said.

Chance nearly groaned at the sensual expression on her face as she savored the food. He forced himself to focus on her comment, instead of the overwhelming urge to lean over the table and cover her mouth with his. "Uh, yes, it is, isn't it. I used to eat here at least twice a week."

"You must really love Italian food—this isn't exactly in your neighborhood," Jennifer commented.

"I taught a few classes here," he told her. "Before I took on a few other medical duties and had to cut back on teaching."

"Did you like doing it? Teaching, I mean?"

"Yeah, I did." He smiled at her, lifting his glass to salute her. "Another thing we have in common—we both like to teach."

Jennifer tipped her glass at him in response and sipped. "I don't know if I'd ever want to teach at the college level," she admitted to him. "I'm more interested in teaching young children."

"An honorable goal," he agreed. "And little kids are a lot of fun. What subject do you see yourself teaching?"

Time slipped by as they ate, drank wine and talked.

The restaurant's crowd was growing thin when Jennifer glanced at her watch and gasped. "Oh, my goodness—look at the time!" She looked at Chance, her expression apologetic. "I really have to go. I'm working the early shift and have to be at the diner by 5:00 a.m. I'll be staggering if I don't get some sleep."

"Much as I hate for the night to end, I don't want to be responsible for you being exhausted tomorrow,"

Chance assured her. He stopped a waiter to request the bill and moments later, they left the restaurant.

Despite needing sleep, Jennifer wished the drive back to her apartment wasn't quite so short.

"Wait," Chance muttered as she twisted her key in the lock of her apartment door.

Jennifer paused, looking up at him, and he bent his head, his mouth covering hers in a kiss.

Sweet, sensual and so arousing that Jennifer's insides melted like warm chocolate, the kiss lured, enticed and made desire and need beat through her veins.

When at last he lifted his mouth from hers, she realized that she was pinned between his hard body and the wall next to her door. The cove of her hips cradled his, the hard proof of his arousal snugged against her abdomen, and the tips of her breasts ached under the pressure of his chest.

"Honey," he rasped against her throat, "it's damned hard to leave you."

She smiled, eyes half-closed at the caress of his lips against her skin when he spoke. "I know," she murmured. "It's hard to let you go." She planted her palms against his shirt and gently pushed.

He retreated a bare half inch, and his head lifted so he could look down into her face.

"But if you don't leave, I won't sleep and that's why you brought me home, remember? So I could sleep." She wasn't sure if she was reminding him— or herself.

"Damn." He sighed, a short gust of air that stirred the tendrils of loose hair curling at her temple. "You're right."

He pressed a final hard kiss against her lips and stepped away from her. The loss of his weight and warmth made her want to grab him and pull him back.

A smile lit his dark eyes and his lips curved in a half smile.

"I know how you feel, honey. If you didn't have to work early tomorrow, I'd kidnap you and take you home to bed." He reached past her and pushed the door partially open. "I'll see you tomorrow at the diner for breakfast."

"Okay," she whispered breathlessly. "Good night."

The door clicked shut behind her and she twisted the lock, sending the dead bolt home.

"Did you have a good time?"

Margaret's voice behind her snapped Jennifer out of her daze.

"Yes." She turned, carrying her books into the kitchen area to drop them on the end of the table. "I had an absolutely lovely time."

Margaret's eyes sparkled behind the lenses of her glasses. "I'm glad—and I'd like to meet the man that put that glow on your face," she teased.

Jennifer laughed. "He's pretty terrific, Margaret."

"Good. It's about time you met someone terrific." The older woman turned to collect her knitting, tucking the length of cable-knit red and cream-colored afghan into her bag. "I'm heading home so you can get to bed. Now what did I do with my book?" She searched and found a paperback mystery stuck between the cushions. She slipped the book into her knitting bag and took out a key chain. "Walk me to the door?"

"Of course." Jennifer freed the dead bolt and opened her apartment, waiting in the doorway while Margaret crossed the hall to unlock and go inside her own home.

"Good night." Margaret lifted her hand and closed the door.

Jennifer waited until she heard the click of the locks sliding home across the hall before closing and securing her own front door.

The apartment was quiet without Margaret's cheery presence. Jennifer turned off the living-room lights and went to her bedroom, switching on the bedside lamp before tiptoeing into Annie's bedroom.

The little girl was sprawled on her back, red-gold curls a tangle on the pillowcase and the blanket half on, half off the bed.

Jennifer straightened the blanket and tucked it in at Annie's waist before leaning over to kiss her daughter's cheek. Annie mumbled and stirred, rolling over to snuggle her face against the soft fur of the stuffed brown bear in her arms.

A surge of love and affection swept over Jennifer. Once again, she was caught off guard and staggered at the depth of her love for her daughter. Annie was a treasure and in so many ways, a constant source of surprise for Jennifer. The little girl enriched her life in ways she'd never envisioned before she became a mother.

And Jennifer loved every one of them.

She moved quietly back into her own room, stripped out of her clothes to take a quick shower, then pulled on her pajamas and climbed into bed and switched off the light.

After a long time, her world now seemed to be full and the future stretched ahead of her, filled with possibilities.

What could possibly go wrong? she thought with a drowsy smile just before she fell asleep.

* * *

Jennifer's sense of well-being and happiness lasted less than twelve hours.

Due to working a split shift at the diner, she was alone in her apartment just before noon the next day. Annie was at school and Jennifer was almost dressed and ready to return for her second four-hour shift, padding about barefoot as she quickly dusted and neatened the rooms after assembling a casserole and tucking it into the refrigerator for Annie's and Margaret's dinner.

A knock on her door interrupted her and, thinking it might be Margaret, she hurried out of the kitchen. A quick glance out the apartment door peephole startled her speechless and she froze, staring at the man who stood outside in the hallway.

"What on earth is *he* doing here?" she murmured to herself, nonplussed.

The man knocked again, an impatient rap of his knuckles against the door panels.

Annoyed, Jennifer threw the dead bolt and yanked open the door. "Hello, Patrick."

"Hello, Jennifer." Her ex-husband smiled, exuding boyish charm.

His endearing smile had no effect on Jennifer.

Fortunately, she thought dispassionately, she'd been well and truly inoculated.

"What are you doing here?" she asked.

"I'd like to talk to you." He peered over her shoulder and gestured at the room behind her. "But I'd rather not have this conversation in the hallway. Won't you ask me in?"

Jennifer narrowed her eyes, studying him. She knew very well that Patrick wanted something but she couldn't imagine what it could be. He'd blithely walked away from their short marriage before Annie was born and hadn't contacted her since.

Nevertheless, whatever he wanted to talk to her about, it was probably best done in the privacy of her apartment.

"Very well, come in." Reluctantly, she stepped back and waved him inside.

"Nice," he commented, his gaze running over the small rooms. "You always did have a natural ability for decorating, Jennifer."

Jennifer ignored the comment, knowing full well his compliments were always charmingly insincere. "I have to leave for work, Patrick, so maybe you can cut to the chase and just tell me why you're here."

His gaze sharpened with swift annoyance and then

he shrugged, his expression bland once more. "You always were appallingly direct, Jennifer."

"I prefer to call it being honest," she told him. "So…?"

"Very well." He reached into the inner pocket of his suit jacket and took out a newspaper clipping, handing it to Jennifer.

She unfolded the newsprint, frowning when she saw it was the photo of her and Chance, dancing at the Founder's Ball, and the accompanying gossip column notation listing their names.

"I'm afraid I don't understand." She looked at him, confused.

"It appears you're dating Dr. Chance Demetrios."

"And if I am?" Jennifer couldn't imagine where this conversation was going. Granted, she hadn't dated anyone since the divorce but surely Patrick wouldn't care if she went out with someone.

"I don't know if you're aware, but I've finished med school and completed my internship."

"Congratulations." She eyed him, waiting, wishing he'd get to the point.

"I'm applying for various positions—including an opening in the research department at the Armstrong Fertility Institute."

Jennifer stared at him, beginning to guess where

the conversation was going. "And you're telling me this…why?"

"Dr. Demetrios and his partner are doing cutting-edge research in his field. I want to be a part of that research team."

Slow anger began to churn in Jennifer's midsection. "What does this have to do with me?"

Patrick smiled, shaking his head at her. "Jennifer, Jennifer," he chided. "I'm sure you can see my point. I want you to use your influence with your boyfriend to move my name to the top of the hiring list."

"No." Jennifer shoved the newspaper clipping into his hand. "If that's all you wanted to talk to me about, I really have to get to work." She walked to the door.

"How's Annie?"

Jennifer froze, hand on the doorknob, then slowly turned to stare at him. "I'm surprised you know her name."

"Of course I know her name," he said, faintly reproachful. "After all, she's my daughter."

Unease shivered up Jennifer's spine. "I thought we resolved your connection to Annie when you agreed to give me full custody in return for my not asking for child support. You've never shown any interest in her before."

"That's true," he agreed blandly. "But I've been re-thinking my position as her father. I'm wondering if I shouldn't ask the court to set up a visitation schedule so I can get to know my daughter."

"You don't want to get to know Annie," Jennifer told him, coldly furious. "You're using her to threaten me so I'll ask Chance to hire you."

"You always were quick to grasp the basics," he conceded. "I don't want to take you back to court and force you to let me have Annie for alternate weekends. If I were involved in demanding re-search, perhaps I would be too busy to have her with me, anyway."

"This is blackmail," she said, fighting to keep her words even. Anger warred with worry, threatening to make her voice tremble.

"Blackmail is such a harsh word, Jennifer," he informed her. "I prefer calling this a…negotiation for mutual benefits."

"You've always been good at hiding your selfish interests behind pretty words," she retorted bitterly. "I won't do it, Patrick. I can't do it. Chance and I don't have that kind of relationship but even if we did, I wouldn't ask him to hire someone like you." She pulled open the door and stood back. "Now get out of my house."

"I suggest you think it over." He moved toward her, stepped into the hallway. "I'll call you soon."

"Please don't," she insisted. "My mind isn't going to change."

He merely smiled and walked down the hall.

Jennifer closed the door with quiet force and threw the dead bolt before she turned, the solid door panel supporting her when she slumped.

Eventually she'd learned Patrick hid a snake's personality behind the charming, handsome facade. Their divorce had certainly shown her a side of him that was unattractive and selfish, but threatening her with Annie's welfare if she didn't help him use Chance to further his career…well, it was beyond belief, even for Patrick.

Glancing at the clock again, she realized more time had slipped away than she'd realized.

"And now I'm going to be late for work," she grumbled, hurrying to the bedroom to grab her shoes.

She wasn't sure how she was going to stop Patrick without endangering Annie, but she was determined to do so.

Jennifer was certain that the day that began with the unexpected visit from her ex-husband could not get any more complicated.

Never had she been so wrong.

* * *

Midafternoon found Chance pushing open the door to the diner and striding inside, pausing to swiftly scan the long room. He didn't see Jennifer and a wave of disappointment washed over him.

Damn. He scanned the room again, slower this time, but still didn't see Jennifer's blond hair.

Enthusiasm dampened, he took a step toward his usual booth but paused abruptly, his gaze sharpening. A little girl sat in the back booth where he'd often seen Jennifer studying on her breaks. The child's head was bent over a book lying open atop the table, long red-gold curls falling forward over her shoulder as she focused intently on the crayon she moved over the page.

She looked up, her gaze unerringly finding his as if she'd felt his stare. Chance went still—he knew those deep blue eyes. They were duplicates of Jennifer's—same color, same shape beneath the arch of delicate brows. He had an instant mental image of a small curl of red hair tucked into the silver locket he'd found in his sheets after the unforgettable night Jennifer had spent in his bed. This child's hair had the same sheen of glossy, burnished red-gold. And the pixie face framed by that mane of curls was the same as in the locket's tiny photo.

Intrigued, he immediately changed direction.

"Hi, there," he said when he reached the back booth.

The little girl studied him gravely, her blue eyes inspecting him with curiosity. "Hi." Her childish voice was a clear treble. "Who are you?"

"I'm Chance. Who are you?"

"Annie."

"Nice to meet you, Annie. You have blue eyes just like my friend Jennifer. Do you know Jennifer?"

"That's my mom!" A smile lit her face and she beamed up at him. "I'm waiting for her till she gets off work."

"I see." Despite his suspicions, Chance was stunned when the little girl cheerfully confirmed his guess. Jennifer had a child and she'd never told him. In fact, she'd never even mentioned being a mother. Why not? Was she keeping the child a secret? He glanced at the papers and books spread out over the tabletop. "What are you doing?"

"Coloring."

He tilted his head to better view the page under her hand. "Nice," he commented. The ballgown on the drawing of a gold-crowned princess matched the magenta crayon in her hand. "Who is she?"

"She's a princess and her name is Cinderella,"

Annie told him with a reproving stare. "Don't you know a princess when you see one?"

"Uh, well…" Amused and charmed, he shrugged, a smile tugging at the corners of his mouth. "I thought I did, but maybe not."

She pointed a small, imperious finger at the seat opposite her. "I know all about princesses. If you sit down, I'll tell you. Princesses are important."

Intrigued and entertained, Chance slid onto the bench seat and propped his elbows on the table.

"I'm guessing you're a princess, right?" he asked.

"Sometimes." She nodded.

"And what about your mom—is she a princess, too?"

"No," she said promptly. "She's a queen."

"Yes," Chance agreed. He had a quick mental image of blond hair, long legs, graceful carriage and wise eyes. "She certainly is," he added softly.

Chapter Five

Jennifer left the restroom and returned to the diner's main room just in time to see Chance standing next to the booth where she'd left Annie. Stunned, she froze for a moment, staring with disbelief as Chance leaned slightly forward to look at Annie's coloring book, the two exchanging words. Then Annie pointed at the seat opposite and Chance slid onto the bench to join her.

Oh, no, Jennifer nearly groaned aloud. Once again, Chance was sweeping aside an iron-clad rule she'd established for her life. He was like a force of nature and, apparently, virtually unstoppable.

Jennifer started toward the two, determined to send him on his way, out of her daughter's booth and firmly outside Annie's small sphere of male influences. Unfortunately, her progress was stopped by customers. Filling four different requests for coffee delayed her and it was ten minutes later before she reached Annie's booth.

"Hi, Mommy." A smile lit Annie's pixie face and she beamed up at Jennifer. Dressed in a navy-blue school jumper with a white blouse and pink sweater, the little girl's legs and small feet in black Mary Jane shoes were tucked beneath her as she knelt on the red vinyl seat. The crayons lay scattered now, clearly forgotten as she'd chatted with the big man seated opposite her. "Chance likes dogs, too."

"Call him Dr. Demetrios, Annie." Jennifer's gaze met Chance's, momentarily distracted by Annie's unexpected comment.

His dark eyes sparked with amusement. "I suggested a rottweiler like Butch or a Great Pyrenees but Annie seems to be leaning toward something bigger."

"Bigger?" Jennifer felt her eyes widen. "What could possibly be bigger?"

"A Newfie," Annie told her with conviction. "I really like Newfoundlands, Mommy. They have the sweetest faces and kind eyes. I saw a picture of one in a book." She switched her gaze to Chance. "I go to school and my teacher takes us to the library," she said confidingly.

"Pretty cool teacher," he agreed with a grin. "Especially if the library has dog books with pictures."

"Oh, yes," she assured him. "It has lots of dog books—I counted four." She looked back at Jennifer. "I think we should get a black Newfoundland and name her Sadie."

"Sadie's a very nice name," Jennifer conceded. "And Newfoundlands are known for being even-tempered and sweet-natured dogs but, honey—" she paused, mentally picturing a very, very large dog "—I think they weigh over a hundred pounds. I'm not sure she would fit, even if we had a house with a yard. Maybe you should consider a smaller breed, like a miniature dachshund or a Chihuahua."

"I don't think so, Mommy," Annie replied, her expression serious as she leaned forward to peer up at her mother. "I think we need a big watchdog. 'Cause we don't have a daddy that lives with us to keep us safe from burglars and things."

Startled speechless, Jennifer could only stare as she tried to think of a reasoned reply. But she drew a blank. "I didn't know you worried about burglars, Annie."

"I don't so much," Annie said blithely. "But until we find us a daddy, we should have a dog."

Jennifer felt her eyes go round. She glanced at Chance and found him watching her. His mouth wasn't curved upward but laughter danced in his dark eyes. She frowned at him and he grinned, lifting his hands as if to disclaim any responsibility for Annie's comments.

"When did you decide this?" she asked Annie, turning away from Chance so she couldn't see his amusement at what must have been obvious astonishment on her face. She wasn't going to admit that Annie had taken her completely by surprise. Not that it would have done her any good to deny it since she was sure her expression must have been clear enough.

"Today at school. Melinda said she'd share her daddy but I think we should get one of our own." A small, worried frown creased her brow. "Do you think it will be hard to find one that likes Newfoundland dogs?" She turned to Chance, leaning on her elbows to get closer. "What do you think, Chance?"

"I think any man worth his salt would like to have a Newfoundland dog named Sadie." He bent forward to lean his forearms on the tabletop and the move narrowed the distance between them across the table to barely a foot. "And if the package included a little red-haired girl named Annie, it would be a deal too good to turn down."

Annie beamed at him with approval before turning to Jennifer. "See, Mommy? We're a good deal."

"You and Sadie certainly would be," Jennifer agreed. She glanced at her wristwatch. "My shift is finished and it's time for us to head home. Why don't you put your things away in your backpack while I go get my purse and jacket."

"Okay."

Jennifer switched her attention to Chance and opened her mouth to say goodbye but he spoke first.

"I've got my car outside. I'll give you a lift home."

"That's a lovely offer, Chance, but Annie can't ride in a car without a child's safety seat and I'm sure you don't…"

"You can borrow the one out of my car," Linda interrupted eagerly, slowing on her way past them with a tray of dishes. She paused, balancing the tray on one hip while she fished a key ring from her pocket. "Here you are, Chance. It's the blue sedan parked directly across the street."

"But…" Jennifer protested. Linda merely winked at her.

"Thanks, Linda." Chance took the key and stood.

"I'll be right back, you two." He leveled his index finger at Jennifer. "Wait for me."

"Well, I…"

Annie tugged at her arm. "Please, Mommy," she whispered loudly. "I don't want to ride the bus today. I want to go with Chance."

"Dr. Demetrios," Jennifer corrected absentmindedly, giving in to the plea in Annie's blue eyes. "All right." She glanced at Chance. "We'll be here."

Chance didn't wait for Jennifer to say anything more. He left the diner and jogged across the street to Linda's sedan. It only took a few moments to remove the safety seat from the rear of Linda's vehicle but it took a bit longer to install it in the back of his Jaguar. As he adjusted the seat belt, he thought about the little girl. Damned if he didn't like the kid, he thought with a rueful grin. She'd chattered nonstop, her conversation about her love of all things Disney Princess–connected and her desire for a large dog interspersed with questions. He'd been downright charmed by her and had given her answers to blunt questions that he would have adroitly avoided had she been twenty years older.

Annie seemed to have the same effect on him as her mother, he reflected as he jogged back across the street. None of the usual rules applied to them.

He found the little red-haired girl enchanting. And she seemed equally pleased with him.

And how crazy is that? he thought as he pushed open the door and reentered the diner. He didn't dislike kids, exactly, but he'd never had a particular interest in them, either. Until Annie.

"Do you ladies have plans for dinner?" he asked as they drove away from the diner. "I've been craving pizza all day—not just any pizza, but my favorite pizza at Giovanni's."

"I love pizza!" Annie exclaimed from the backseat.

"That makes two of us who vote for pizza. How about you, Jennifer?" Chance inquired when she remained silent. "Do you love pizza?"

She glanced sideways at him, her expression closed, her eyes wary. "I like pizza," she confirmed. "But I have a casserole in the fridge for dinner tonight, and I have to be at class at six-thirty so I'm afraid we can't—"

"Please, Mommy," Annie pleaded. "I really, really want to have pizza. We can have the casserole tomorrow night."

"I'm not sure we have time to go out for dinner, Annie. I have to take you home, then go to class…"

"I'll drive you," Chance put in. "It would be my pleasure."

She gave him an uncertain look.

"But if you truly can't make it tonight, then I'll take you home and wait while you settle Annie before driving you to the campus," he told her. "We can go out for pizza another time."

"Well, I…" Her fingers worried the strap of her purse in her lap.

Chance felt like a heel. She clearly was torn and though he didn't know why, her concern was obviously focused on his invitation to dinner. "I didn't mean to pressure you, Jennifer," he murmured. He covered her hands with his for one brief squeeze of reassurance. "Don't worry about it. Just tell me what you want to do."

He braked for a red light and looked at her to find her gaze on him, intent. Stiffly held shoulders slowly relaxed and she nodded with decision.

"Pizza sounds good—and Annie's right, the casserole will keep until tomorrow night."

"Great." He grinned at her and Annie's whoop of delight in the backseat had Jennifer smiling back. "Giovanni's restaurant is only a couple of blocks from here."

The light turned green and he switched his attention to the street, weaving expertly through traffic before he slotted the sleek Jaguar into a parking spot.

The moment they exited the car a short half block

from the restaurant, the wonderful smell of yeasty bread and Italian sauce reached them. And when Chance held the door wide and ushered Jennifer and Annie into the restaurant, the aroma surrounded them.

"It smells yummy in here," Annie whispered loudly as they took seats.

"I think that's one of the reasons I like coming here," Chance told her.

"I love it," Annie proclaimed with a definitive nod.

"Well, I guess that's the seal of approval," Chance indicated to Jennifer.

She rolled her eyes at him. "Annie's nothing if not decisive. I suspect she'll grow up to be the first female president of the United States. Or maybe CEO of Häagen-Dazs since she loves the ice cream and she'd get free samples."

Chance laughed out loud, drawing indulgent smiles from surrounding tables.

The spontaneous late-afternoon meal went by too quickly. After dropping Annie off at home in the care of Margaret, Chance drove Jennifer to the campus and all too soon, it was time to say goodbye.

"Thanks for coming to dinner with me," he told her. "Your daughter is terrific. I enjoyed getting to know her."

A tiny frown drew the feathery arches of Jennifer's brows into a vee. "About Annie, Chance…" She paused, seeming to search for words.

"What about Annie?" he prompted. Without thinking, he smoothed his thumb over the little worry lines between her brows, his fingers trailing down the line of her cheek and jaw in a lingering caress. Her skin was silky soft beneath his hand and a rush of fierce emotion shook him. He could deal with lust—he expected it. But this feeling of protective affection, this was something else.

"I haven't dated, mostly, because I didn't want Annie getting attached to men who were just casual friends," she explained. "I didn't want her to get hurt."

"So I'm the first guy she's seen with you since the divorce."

"You're the first man she's seen with me, period. Her father and I were divorced before she was born and he's never met her."

Chance bit off a curse. "You mean to tell me that little girl's daddy isn't part of her life?" He was incredulous.

"Patrick was furious when I told him I was pregnant. He'd never wanted children. He moved out that night and filed for divorce within a week."

He tried to assimilate the blunt words. "What an ass," he said finally.

"Yes, he was." Her mouth quirked and she smiled at him, eyes sparkling.

"Jennifer…" He cupped her chin in his palm, his gaze holding hers. "Some men are just brainless. But I'm not—and I'd never harm Annie or you. I'm not sure what this is between us but I'd cut off my arm before I'd see either one of you hurt."

Her blue eyes misted. "You're a good man, Chance Demetrios," she said softly.

"Hell, no, I'm not." He kissed her, savoring the sweetness of her mouth as her lips softened beneath his and she kissed him back.

When at last he lifted his head, her hands clutched his shirt and they were both breathing hard.

"Can I wait and give you a ride home?" he asked.

"No, thanks," she murmured. "This is the night our class lets out early and one of my study group members gives me a ride home. She says she doesn't mind dropping me, even though it's out of her way, because it gives us a little longer to study."

Reluctantly, Chance let her go. She turned at the doorway to wave, then disappeared inside the lecture hall.

She hadn't been completely convinced that both she and Annie's hearts were safe with him, he thought as he drove away.

I could have told her I think I'm falling in love with her, he thought somberly. *That might have reassured her.*

But he wasn't sure he was ready to admit he'd finally met the one woman who could turn him inside out and stand his world on end. Even to himself.

"Put your pajamas on, sweetie," Jennifer called as she blotted water from the bathroom floor the following evening. She made a mental note to toss a couple of towels on the tile tomorrow night before Annie took her bath. The child splashed water as if she were a dolphin in a pool.

She wondered if Chance was still in his office at the institute. He'd called earlier in the day to say he had to work late that night but wanted to invite her and Annie on a picnic the following Saturday. She'd been surprised by the depth of disappointment she'd felt that she wouldn't be seeing him sooner but decided it was probably a perfectly normal reaction. She hadn't dated anyone in so long she could hardly remember what constituted "normal."

She dropped the damp towels in the hamper and folded Annie's crumpled jeans and T-shirt, laying them on the counter next to the sink.

"Annie," she yelled in an attempt to hurry her

daughter. "As soon as you're dressed, we'll pop over to Margaret's apartment to see how she's feeling."

"Okay." Annie appeared in the doorway, her voice muffled as she pulled the top to a pair of pink princess pajamas over her head. Her mop of soft curls was damp, curling wildly around her face. "Margaret coughed a lot this afternoon, Mommy."

"Did she?" Jennifer hung the wet towel over a bar, cast a quick glance around the neat bathroom, and joined Annie. "That's why we're going to go check on her."

Annie dashed ahead of her, waiting for Jennifer to slide the dead bolt free before they crossed the hall. When Margaret didn't immediately answer the doorbell, Annie knocked on the door panel. When at last Margaret opened the door, Jennifer understood the delay. Her neighbor's face was pale, the only color a faint flush over her cheekbones, and her mouth was taut with distress.

"Margaret, my goodness." She took the older woman's arm and steadied her, concern heightening when she felt the usually spry body tremble and lean heavily. "Annie, come in and close the door," she commanded, waiting until the little girl had done so before she guided Margaret to a seat on the sofa. "How long have you…" She was interrupted when the older woman began to cough, a hacking, painful sound in the quiet apartment.

Jennifer laid her palm on Margaret's forehead. "You feel warm. Have you taken your temperature—do you have a fever?"

"Just a slight one," Margaret responded, her voice weak and faintly raspy.

"That's it," Jennifer said with decision. "You need to see a doctor."

"No, no," Margaret protested but with a distinct lack of her usual energy and forcefulness. "I'm sure it's just a cold and I'll be fine in a day or two."

"Maybe." Jennifer was unconvinced. "I certainly hope you're right. But in the meantime, let's have a doctor at the free clinic check you out, just to be sure." Her gaze met Margaret's. "I don't like the sound of that cough, nor the fact that you're running a temp. If you need an antibiotic, the sooner it's started, the better."

Margaret sighed. "Very well."

Her easy capitulation worried Jennifer even more. Margaret was too compliant and very unlike her usual self. As she helped the older woman dress, even tying her shoes, Jennifer became even more concerned.

"We need to make a quick stop in our apartment so Annie and I can grab a light sweater—and I need my purse," Jennifer said as she collected Margaret's apartment keys and purse, locking up behind them.

"Mommy, do I get to wear my pajamas outside?" Annie asked as Jennifer unlocked the door to her own apartment and helped Margaret inside.

"Why don't you pull on jeans over your jammies," Jennifer suggested. "Or just change clothes—but hurry, we don't want to keep the cab waiting."

"Take the money for the cab out of my wallet," Margaret told her, eyes closing as she laid her head back against the sofa.

Jennifer would have insisted on paying herself but she knew Margaret would argue and the older woman seemed too weary.

"Of course, Margaret, I'll do that," she agreed, catching up a sweater from where it hung on the back of a kitchen chair. It took only a moment to collect her purse from the bedroom and she hurried back into the living room. "Annie," she called. "Are you ready?"

"Yes, Mommy." The little girl appeared, dressed in laced-up sneakers, jeans, a T-shirt and pink sweater. She carried her backpack, bulging at the seams.

Jennifer glanced at her watch. "Great, let's head downstairs. The cab should be here soon."

Luck was with them, for they'd barely reached the

exit to the street when a cab pulled up to the curb, lights bright.

"Thank goodness," Jennifer murmured. She handed Margaret into the cab, Annie scrambled inside and Jennifer gave the driver the address for the free clinic.

Dusk was falling and streetlights glowed outside the medical offices. Jennifer helped Margaret climb the three shallow steps to the entry as the cab drove away. Annie walked beside them, uncharacteristically quiet. Backpack slung over her shoulder, she grabbed the handle with both hands and with an effort, pushed the heavy door inward, holding it while the two women made their way into the reception area.

The room was nearly empty. Only two other people sat there—a young woman with a crying baby in her arms and an elderly gentleman sucking on an unlit pipe.

Jennifer helped Margaret to a seat on a vinyl-covered sofa against the wall and Annie sat next to her, eyeing the woman and small baby with concerned interest.

"Good evening." The receptionist smiled when Jennifer walked to the counter. "What can we do for you?"

"My neighbor has a bad cough and a temperature. She needs to see a doctor." Jennifer looked over her shoulder when Margaret began to cough, the sound grating.

"I think we can get her in quickly," the receptionist assured her. "The doctor is in with a patient now, and the other folks here are waiting for test results to come back so it should only be a few moments. I'll need you to fill out a form with her personal stats and insurance information."

The paperwork took only a few moments and once finished, Jennifer joined Margaret on the sofa, Annie tucked between them.

"It shouldn't be too long, Margaret," she began. "The receptionist said the doctor was…"

The door to the inner rooms opened and a young man exited, his hand wrapped in thick white bandages. A tall, dark-haired man in a white lab coat followed him.

"Next time, try to be more careful when you're slicing vegetables," the doctor said.

"Thanks, Doc, I will."

Jennifer stared at the doctor, blinking in disbelief. The voice she knew so well, the face she saw in her dreams and the doctor who worked in the halls of the Armstrong Fertility Institute was here.

What was Chance Demetrios doing in the free clinic? It was the last place she'd expected to see him.

"Look, Mommy, it's Chance." Annie hopped off the sofa and dashed across the tile floor.

"Hey, Annie." Chance grinned at her. "What are you doing here?" The smile disappeared and he looked up, scanning the room. His features cleared when his gaze met Jennifer's and he walked toward her. "Hello, Jennifer."

"Hi." She stood. "I didn't expect to see you here."

"I work here," he said simply. "Why are you here—are you and Annie okay?"

"Oh, we're fine," she assured him quickly. "It's Margaret, our neighbor."

On the sofa, the older woman stirred, opening her eyes and sitting up straighter.

"I see," Chance said. "You must be Margaret," he told her, his voice gentle, his eyes assessing. "Why don't we get you into an exam room?"

He helped her to stand, his big hand cupping her elbow.

He glanced over his shoulder. "You can come with us, Jennifer. You, too, Annie."

They followed down a short hallway, slowly as Chance let Margaret set the pace. When she was settled on an exam table, he gestured for Jennifer to take a seat on the single, straight-backed wooden chair in the small room.

Annie perched on her mother's lap, her eyes bright, round as she watched Chance.

"So, what's going on, Margaret?" he queried, wrapping a blood pressure cuff around her thin upper arm.

"I have a cold," she told him. "Well, it started as a cold," she amended. "But late this afternoon, I noticed I was feeling hot and my thermometer confirmed I had a temperature."

"I see." Chance noted the blood pressure stats and removed the cuff from her arm. "There's a lot of flu going around," he informed her. "Let's check your temperature. Hmm," he said a moment later. "It is a little elevated."

Margaret nodded, clearly weary. "I thought so."

Jennifer managed to contain her worry until Chance had finished his examination.

"Does she have the flu?" she asked when he began making notes on a chart.

"I'm afraid so," he told her. "I'd like to have her spend the night in the hospital. We'll give her fluids and watch her to be sure the she doesn't get worse."

"I don't want to go to the hospital," Margaret argued, a hint of her normal asperity in her weary voice.

"I know you don't," Jennifer assured her gently. "But a single night being cared for is better than having you go home, get worse, and then perhaps face several days in the hospital."

"True." Margaret's response was grudgingly agreeing.

"You're doing the wise thing," Chance stated, patting her thin shoulder. "I'll make arrangements for transporting you to City General. I'll be right back."

"I'd much rather go home. I don't like hospitals," Margaret grumbled, lying back on the exam table as the door closed on Chance's back.

"I know," Jennifer soothed. "And I don't blame you but I think Dr. Demetrios is right—you've made the wise choice."

"Perhaps," she said wearily.

Chance returned shortly, his presence seeming to fill the room. "Your ride is here, Mrs. Sullivan."

"Goodness, that was fast." Margaret peered owlishly up at him. "Are you a magician?"

"No, ma'am." He smile flashed, his teeth white in his suntanned face. "An ambulance was in the neighborhood when my receptionist put in a call for transport. I think we just got lucky here."

"Good," Margaret murmured. "It's about time. I could use some luck."

"I suspect we'd all like a little more luck," Chance told her.

Voices sounded in the hall outside and Chance pulled open the exam-room door. "The patient is in here," he called. "The EMTs are going to need room so let's step outside, Jennifer, Annie."

"We'll see you tomorrow morning, Margaret," Jennifer promised, bending to brush a quick kiss against the older woman's pale cheek.

"Me, too, Margaret." Annie carefully followed her mother's example with a brief kiss. "We love you, Margaret."

A smile lifted the corners of Margaret's mouth. "I love you, too, sweetie."

Her eyes drifted closed as Annie stepped back. Jennifer took her hand, following Chance into the hallway to make room for the two ambulance attendants and their gurney. The pair quickly and efficiently transferred Margaret to the stretcher, tucking a blanket around her small frame and strapping her securely.

"See you tomorrow, Margaret," Annie repeated as the two men wheeled her down the hallway to the exit and their waiting ambulance. Her fingers clutched Jennifer's and when the back door closed, she turned her worried face up to her mother's. "She's going to be okay, isn't she, Mommy?"

"Chance says she will be and he's a very good doctor, honey," Jennifer reassured her, smoothing

her palm over the silky mop of curls in uncon-
scious comfort.

Annie's blue gaze switched to Chance, questioning.

He dropped to his heels in front of her. "Your
friend is going to be just fine, Annie. The nurses at
the hospital will keep watch over her tonight and
she'll get medicine so that she can come home in the
morning. Okay?"

"Okay." Annie's cupid mouth tilted in a brief
smile and Chance's big hand cupped her small chin
for a moment.

Then he stood, his gaze soothing as he met
Jennifer's.

"I'll pick you up around ten tomorrow morning
and you two can come to the hospital with me. I have
to do rounds to check on several patients and you can
visit with Margaret until I'm finished. Then I'll give
you all a ride home."

"Thank you," she said simply. She might have
declined, given her determination to be independent,
but it would be much better for Margaret if Chance
chauffeured them home in his comfortable car.

"I'd take you and Annie home tonight but my shift
doesn't end for several hours. I had my receptionist
call a cab—it's waiting outside," he told her. His gaze
flicked assessingly over Annie's face. "I know you

could take the bus but humor me. It's late and Annie looks like she's about to fall asleep on her feet."

Jennifer knew Annie was tired. The weight of her small body leaned against her side and the hour was way past her usual bedtime.

"All right."

Relief spread over his features and he smiled at her with such warmth that her knees went weak.

"Thanks," he murmured as he walked them down the hallway, through the reception area and out to the waiting cab. "I'll feel better knowing the cab will take you straight home."

"Good night, Chance." Annie's farewell was interrupted by a jaw-cracking yawn as she slid onto the worn leather seat.

"Good night, and thank you, Chance," Jennifer said.

"I'll see you in the morning," he promised.

For a moment, she thought he was going to kiss her, but then he closed the door. He leaned in the open window of the cab's passenger front seat.

"Take good care of my girls," he indicated, handing the driver folded bills.

"You bet," the driver replied, taking the currency.

Chance stepped back and the cab pulled away from the curb.

His girls? Jennifer wasn't sure how she felt about

the possessive note in Chance's voice. But affection for the big man and his obvious concern for her, Annie and Margaret curled warmly through her body. It had been a long time since anyone made her feel so cared for and she liked it, maybe too much, she thought soberly.

Was she coming to depend too much on Chance's place in her life? And if she was, how painful would it be when he moved on, as surely he would?

She pushed the thoughts aside, determined not to spoil the happiness she felt with Chance today by worrying about the future.

The following morning, as promised, Chance collected Jennifer and Annie and took them to the hospital with him. They dashed through the rain from the car to the double-doored entrance, their jackets quickly growing damp from the spring storm. He left them on Margaret's floor, promising to collect them in an hour or so.

Fortunately, Margaret was feeling much better and by the time they returned to their apartment building to settle the elderly woman into her own bed, it was well past noon.

"Are you sure Margaret is okay by herself?" Annie asked, her little face worried. "Maybe she should come stay with us till she's all better."

"She wants to rest in her own bed, honey," Jennifer told her. "But we're just across the hall so we can run in and out often to make sure she's all right and has everything she needs."

"Like lunch?" Annie climbed onto a kitchen chair and leaned on her elbows. "I'm hungry. I bet Margaret is, too."

"She had an early lunch at the hospital, remember?" Jennifer recalled. "But we didn't so I'm not surprised you're hungry. What would you like for lunch?"

"How about Chinese?" Chance put in. "I noticed there's a take-out place on the corner."

"Yeah! I love Chinese food," Annie instantly crowed with approval.

Chance leaned against the counter, arms crossed over his chest, and cocked an eyebrow at Jennifer. "How about you? Do you love Chinese food?"

"Yes, but you'll soon learn that Annie claims she loves all kinds of ethnic food, whether she's actually tasted it or not," Jennifer said dryly.

"Good, that simplifies matters," he told her. "Do you have a take-out menu for the restaurant?"

Jennifer pointed past his shoulder. "There's one on the fridge."

A half hour later, they sat around the table, a dozen boxes of food opened and plates in front of them.

"I like this stuff," Annie proclaimed. "What is it?"

Chance leaned over to inspect the bite of food on her fork. "That's almond chicken," he informed her.

"It's yummy."

He grinned at Jennifer. "She likes it."

"I guess we can add it to the short list of ethnic food she's actually tried," Jennifer decided.

"I want to use chopsticks, too," Annie said.

"A fork is lots easier to eat with," her mother insisted.

"Chance uses chopsticks."

"True." He glanced at Jennifer for permission, waiting until she nodded before he tore the wrapping off a pair of plastic chopsticks from the restaurant and handed them to Annie. She held them awkwardly, stabbing a piece of chicken but dropping it before it reached her mouth. "Not that way," Chance instructed. "Here, I'll show you."

He stood, rounding the table to lean over her, moving her little fingers to properly grip the two sticks, then helping her pick up a bite.

Jennifer clapped when the small piece of chicken disappeared into Annie's mouth and her eyes lit with success.

"Look, Mommy," she said, her mouth full of chicken. "I can use chopsticks."

"Yes, you certainly can." Jennifer exchanged a mutually amused look with Chance.

Outside, the rain came down, pattering against the windowpanes and watering the spring flowers and budding trees. Inside, the three of them finished lunch, neatened the kitchen and then settled around the coffee table for a game of Clue. Jennifer switched on the CD player and the raspy voice of Louis Armstrong sang the lyrics of a 1940s blues tune. She lowered the volume until the music was a pleasant background, adding to the apartment's cozy, comfortable air.

Chance rolled the dice and moved his playing piece on the board.

"Oh, no," Annie groaned dramatically. "You're in the library and with Miss Scarlet!"

Chance laughed. "I haven't played this game since I was a kid but I seem to remember that when a fellow player doesn't want me landing in a room, it probably means she knows something about who killed who."

Annie gave him an impish look. "Maybe, maybe not." She tossed her head, her ponytail of red-gold hair gleaming in the lamplight. "I'll never tell."

Jennifer leaned sideways to whisper loudly. "I should warn you—Annie almost always wins this game."

"Aha. Now you've challenged me," he told them. "This is serious. I have to win to prove guys can play this game well, too." He gave the two females a fierce frown and they laughed, identical blue eyes sparkling with merriment.

Damn, he realized with sudden insight. *I'm having fun, playing a board game with a kid and her mom.* Nothing could be further from the polished, sexually willing debutantes and black-tie events that had often been the focus of his past social life. Was it possible his conviction that he wasn't wired for family life was only because he'd never met the right woman? The thought was startling—and he shoved it to the back of his mind, to be considered later. Maybe much later. At the moment, he was enjoying himself too much to ponder weightier subjects.

Later that evening, when Chance had left the apartment and Annie was asleep, snuggled beneath the pink princess coverlet on her bed, Jennifer curled up in her own.

The lamplight cast a circle of gold light over the book on her lap and the notebook with her pen. She'd planned to study but kept thinking about the afternoon just past.

There was such a disparity between Chance's playboy image and the man who'd sat cross-legged on her floor, arguing spiritedly with her daughter over who was the culprit in their game of Junior Clue.

A smile curved her mouth, her eyes going unfocused as she replayed the scene in her mind's eye. In some ways, the afternoon had been bittersweet because it had created an image for her of what life would have been like had Annie's father been a man she could have loved and respected. And if he had been an honorable man who had remained in their lives, she thought.

The phone rang, startling her out of her reverie. She leaned sideways to pick up the portable from the bedside table.

"Hello?"

"Hi, Jennifer."

She almost groaned as she recognized Patrick's voice. "Hello, Patrick."

"I'm calling to check back with you. Have you thought about my request?"

"I told you, Patrick, I'm not going to ask Chance to give you a job."

"I'm sorry to hear that," he said smoothly. "Perhaps we can discuss it further over coffee tomorrow."

"No, I don't think so. Frankly, Patrick, we have nothing to discuss."

"Oh, but we do." His voice turned harder. "We can

certainly leave it to our attorneys but I thought you might want to discuss arranging a visitation schedule in private, just between the two of us. Before my attorney asks for a court date to resolve the issue."

"You have absolutely no interest in seeing Annie," she argued, anger sharpening her tone.

"But I have the right to visit," he told her, "if I choose to exercise that right."

"Fine," she conceded. "I can meet you before I start work."

She gave him the address of a nearby Starbucks and rang off, her fingers trembling as she returned the phone to its base.

Chapter Six

Jennifer was still angry when she walked into the Starbucks the following morning.

Her ex-husband sat at a small round table near the back. He stood, waving at her when she entered. She threaded her way through the tables, the crowd of prework customers thinned at midmorning.

Patrick held her chair before taking his own seat, fastidiously straightening the crease in his suit slacks when he sat. "I ordered a low-fat vanilla latte for you," he told her with a friendly smile. "I remember you used to like them."

"Thank you." She'd vowed to remain polite and to use this meeting to elicit information and gauge Patrick's determination to follow through with his threat. She still had no intention of complying with his request to ask Chance to help his job search. Nevertheless, she didn't want him to start legal proceedings and threaten the stability of Annie's life. She sipped the coffee, eyeing him over the rim of her paper cup. "I confess, Patrick, I'm curious as to how you located me. The newspaper photo and brief comments about my being Chance's guest at the institute's ball didn't list anything about me except my name."

"You're correct. I didn't find you through the newspaper photo," Patrick confirmed. "It was the private investigator who gave me the details, including your current address."

"Private investigator?" Jennifer hoped she concealed her surprise.

"Yes. He didn't specifically tell me, but I gathered he was hired by the Demetrios family to check out the background of the woman their son and heir is dating." Patrick's eyes narrowed. "You do realize who Dr. Chance Demetrios is, don't you?"

Jennifer lifted her brow in cool inquiry, refusing to comment.

"You don't know. Jennifer—" he clucked and

shook his head, amused "—you just might be the only woman in Boston who doesn't know that Chance Demetrios is the only son of Jonathon Demetrios and heir to the Demetrios shipping empire."

Stunned, Jennifer's mind moved at whirlwind speed, trying to remember bits and pieces that might have told her Chance was more than a little rich. But his custom-tailored tuxedo, beautifully appointed town house and the luxurious Jaguar car didn't seem to point to a man who had access to ultrarich funds. Surely a doctor in his position would have those things?

"Of course, when the investigator asked me several extremely personal questions about you, I realized the family was taking the situation seriously—your dating Dr. Demetrios, that is." He spread his hands, his expression smug. "Which, of course, was serendipitous."

"Why is that?" she asked evenly, trying to keep a lid on her anger when she wanted to dump her hot latte over his head.

"Because here am I, having recently graduated from med school and filed an application with the Armstrong Fertility Institute. And here are you." He gestured at her. "My ex-wife, dating a man who's very influential at the institute. And between us, a daughter we both want the best for, I'm sure."

"I've told you, I won't introduce you to Chance or try to influence him in any way to help you obtain a position at the institute. You'll have to rely on your own qualifications. Annie and I have nothing to do with your being hired there."

"Perhaps not," he said smoothly. "But you, Annie and me are connected in a very basic way. Perhaps we should discuss our parental duties and whether it's in our daughter's best interests for you to deny me a father's right to visitation."

"You have absolutely no interest in seeing Annie," she said accusingly, her voice scathing. "You never did, so don't pretend you do now."

"Perhaps," he conceded. "But if you choose not to cooperate with me, I'll have my attorney take you back to court and sue for visitation rights—maybe even for custody."

Jennifer felt her body go cold. "You wouldn't dare," she ground out.

"Of course I would," he assured her amiably, his eyes cold. "I intend to have a prestigious position on the Armstrong research team—any way I can get it." He leaned closer, his voice lowering threateningly. "Don't stand in my way, Jennifer."

"You're despicable," she told him, her voice trembling with fury.

He leaned back with an easy shrug. "Call me what you like—as long as you do what I ask. If you don't," he warned her, "make no mistake, I will exercise my parental rights."

Jennifer stood, unable to bear another moment in his company. "I'll have to think about this. I don't know how I could possibly influence Chance since I have no connection to his work. In fact, I'm not even sure what he does at the institute since he doesn't talk about it."

"You don't have to know what he does," Patrick told her, rising. "Just make sure you convince him to arrange to give me the position. I'm willing to give you a couple weeks, maybe a bit more, but then I'll have to pay a visit to my attorney."

Jennifer didn't answer. In truth, she wasn't sure she could have spoken without outright refusing him. So she bit her tongue and walked away, seething.

She couldn't bring herself to ask Chance to hire Patrick. The man was a snake and, besides, she couldn't use Chance, not even to save Annie.

But how could she keep Patrick from gaining access to her daughter?

After the rainy afternoon playing Clue, Chance found himself spending as much time as possible in Jennifer and Annie's company.

Although lust was a constant, slow-burning flame in his gut whenever he was with Jennifer, he found himself unwilling to pressure her to spend the night with him. Instinct told him that he needed to court her, to give her time to come to terms with his presence in her—and Annie's—life.

He knew she'd looked on their date for the Founder's Ball and the night they'd spent together as a one-time thing.

But he was determined to have her in his bed again.

He suspected Jennifer was still struggling to shift her goals for her life and decide how letting him into her world would also allow her to meet her commitment to protect Annie.

With each day that passed, Chance was more convinced that he wasn't going to be a temporary man in Jennifer's life. He was slowly coming to believe that maybe, just maybe, his life would only be complete if Jennifer and Annie were a permanent part of his world.

Just before lunch on Saturday morning, Chance arrived at Jennifer's apartment with Butch.

She pulled open the door, a smile lighting her face when she saw him. Butch bounded over the threshold, wriggling with pleasure.

"Come in," she told Chance, as she bent to give the big dog a hug. He woofed, one deep sound of greeting, and tried to lick her face.

"Mommy? What was that noise?" Annie entered the living room and stopped abruptly, her eyes widening with surprise. "It's a dog!"

"This is Butch," Chance told her. "Butch, say hello to Annie."

Butch planted his rear on the floor and uttered one more deep woof of hello, ears up, big brown eyes trained on Annie with interest.

"Hello, Butch." Annie looked at Chance. "Can I pet him?"

"Sure." He beckoned her closer. "Hold out your hand and let him sniff it."

If the adults had any concerns about the big dog accepting Annie, they were quickly laid to rest. Within moments, dog and child were seated on the floor, Annie's arm around Butch's neck while she murmured in his ear. He watched her with unflagging interest, his eyes bright.

"I'm just making lunch," Jennifer told him. "Would you like to join us?" She led the way into the small kitchen and he followed, making himself at home as he opened a cupboard door to take down a mug, then poured himself coffee.

"Let's pack those sandwiches and take Annie on a picnic at the park near my house," Chance suggested.

Jennifer looked up. He leaned against the island's countertop, coffee mug in hand, his brown eyes warm.

"We can take Butch, too," he continued. "And the Frisbee, of course. I'll teach Annie how to toss it for Butch to catch. He's pretty good," he added with a grin.

"Annie would love it," Jennifer said. "Are you sure you're up for dealing with one very active little girl in a park, with lots of room to run?"

"Are you suggesting I can't keep up with her?" he asked. His appalled, disbelieving expression was undermined by the amusement in his dark eyes.

"I'm saying I doubt I can keep up with her," she corrected him. "But if you're game, I'm willing to give it a try."

"Great." He set down his coffee cup and strode across the kitchen. He wrapped his arms around her and swung her off her feet, planting a hard kiss on her mouth. "I'll go tell Annie and collect Butch." He set her down and glanced at the counter behind her. "Want some help packing the sandwiches?"

"No, I'm good." She shooed him out of the kitchen, shaking her head with affection as she took plastic containers from the pantry.

A half hour later, Chance parked the car outside his house and they unloaded, then set off for the park.

"How far is it to the park, Chance?" Annie asked, dancing backward in front of him.

"Six blocks," he told her.

"Okay." She spun around to skip forward once more, next to Butch.

The big rottweiler paced happily at the end of the leash, sniffing the warm spring air. He responded to Annie's frequent pats with a quick lick of his tongue and a woof of shared excitement.

"They're quite a pair, aren't they?" Jennifer murmured to Chance. "I'm not sure who's the most excited about this outing—Butch or Annie."

"I think it's a draw," Chance told her.

Jennifer glanced sideways at him. He held Butch's leash in one hand, easily controlling the eager big dog. A bright red blanket was tossed over one shoulder and he carried the wicker picnic basket in the other hand. His long legs were encased in faded jeans that clung faithfully to powerful thigh muscles, his feet covered with polished black boots. At his wrist, a Rolex watch glinted in the sunshine, his arms bare below the short sleeves of a navy polo shirt.

Just looking at him made her happy, she realized.

He glanced sideways at her, met her gaze, and lifted a brow in inquiry. "What?" he asked.

"Nothing." She smiled. "I'm just happy."

His dark eyes warmed, heating with slow promise. "Good to know." His voice was deeper, gravelly.

Jennifer shivered in reaction, anticipation curling slow tendrils of heat low in her belly.

"Look, Mommy, it's the park!" Annie's voice rose with delight.

Jennifer wrestled her thought under control and looked ahead. A half block away, the entry to a large expanse of green grass and trees.

"It must be two full blocks, at least," she commented, looking at Chance for confirmation.

He nodded and glanced at Butch. "The park is one of the reasons I bought a home in the neighborhood. If you want a dog, it's good to have a park nearby. Not to mention—" he grinned at her "—a large supply of plastic bags."

"Plastic bags?" she queried, confused.

"For picking up dog poop. It's a city ordinance, punishable by a fine, if owners don't clean up after their dogs."

"Eeww." Annie grimaced, her gaze meeting Chance's. "That's disgusting."

"Nah," he told her. "You just use a plastic bag and

then tie the ends and toss it in the park trash container. No big deal."

Annie looked unconvinced.

"That's part of being a dog owner," Jennifer told her gently. "If you have a pet, you have to take care of it properly."

"Well." The little girl eyes Butch consideringly. "I guess it's worth it." Her small chin tilted with purpose.

"She's so much like you," Chance murmured to Jennifer, low enough to keep Annie from overhearing.

"And that's a good thing, right?"

"Of course," he said promptly. "Conviction, determination, commitment—what's not good about that?"

They turned off the sidewalk, entering the park and following a winding concrete pathway beneath trees rustling with pale green leaves. On both sides of the walk, freshly mowed green lawns were dotted with beds of bright red, yellow, purple and blue flowers.

The park wasn't crowded but quite a few couples and family groups were taking advantage of the warm spring sunshine. They'd gathered on blankets spread on the grass, brightening the green sward with spots of color. Children ran and laughed, many with blue, red or green balloons tied to their wrists.

"Where are we going to have our picnic, Chance?" Annie asked.

"There's a great spot just a little farther," he told her. "It's just off the sidewalk and near the creek."

"Oooh, there's a creek, too? Fun!" She skipped ahead of the adults, keeping pace with Butch who paced happily at the end of his leash.

Her long red curls bounced as she moved, bright tendrils against the white sweater she wore over a pale blue sundress.

"Where does she get all that energy?" Chance said with wry disbelief, watching Annie's nonstop movement.

"I don't know, but I'd give anything to have just a tiny bit of it," Jennifer told him with a grin.

"Kids are pretty amazing, aren't they?"

"I don't know about all of them," she answered. "But I think Annie is. Of course, she's my daughter and I'm probably prejudiced."

"Yeah, you probably are," he told her. "But speaking as an objective bystander, I think you're right."

Impulsively, Jennifer went up on tiptoe and brushed a kiss against his cheek.

"What was that for?" he asked, his eyes heating.

"Just because."

The moment was broken when Butch and Annie came racing back to drop onto the blanket.

"We're hungry, Mommy," Annie declared. "Can Butch have a sandwich, too?"

Jennifer looked at Chance. "Is Butch allowed to eat a peanut butter and jelly sandwich?"

"It will probably stick to the roof of his mouth but he'll love it," Chance replied with a grin.

Jennifer put a sandwich, chips and a fat dill pickle on each plate and passed them out. She hesitated before sitting a paper plate in front of Butch. "What about pickles?" she said dubiously. "Does he like dill pickles?"

"Butch has a cast-iron stomach," Chance said drily. "And anything that's edible, he loves."

"Do you feed him like this all the time?" she asked as they began to eat and Butch wolfed down his food.

"No, he usually gets dry dog food and the occasional piece of meat, or a big bone to chew." He reached over and tucked a stray tendril of blond hair behind her ear, his fingers brushing in a slow caress over her cheek. "The vet told me he can occasionally have people food. It won't hurt him."

"Oh, good." She would have said more but an elderly man walked by, followed by a trio of golden retriever puppies and their mother on leashes.

Butch woofed and started to rise.

"Butch." Chance's voice was quiet. "Down."

The rottweiler dropped back to the blanket but he quivered with excitement. The puppies heard him and tugged free of the older gentleman to gambol near, touching noses to Butch's, crawling and tumbling over the big dog. Their mother was more cautious but friendly.

Annie caught up one of the puppies and hugged the wriggly, warm body close. "Mommy, I want a puppy like this one."

"Honey, you want a puppy like every one you see," Jennifer chided her with a smile.

Chance and Jennifer helped the elderly man disentangle the darling puppies from Butch and finally he hobbled off down the path toward the bridge across the pond.

"Can we throw the Frisbee for Butch now?" Annie asked when only crumbs were left on the blanket where they sat.

Stretched out beside the little girl, the big dog lifted his head inquiringly when he heard her say his name.

"Sure," Chance answered. He looked at Jennifer. "If your mom says it's okay."

"Fine with me." Jennifer smiled fondly as the three left the blanket, Annie darting ahead, Butch trotting after her, with Chance ambling behind. He'd automatically deferred to her for permission to release Annie to play, she thought, and how nice was that?

"Morning."

Chance looked up from his desk. His partner, Ted Bonner, stood in the doorway, a steaming cup of coffee in his hand. His hair was mussed as if he'd been running his hands through it. The two had gone to Stanford med school together—Chance recognized the signs of frustration.

"Morning. Come in, close the door and tell me what's wrong," he told him.

"What makes you think something's wrong?" Ted closed the door and strolled into the room, dropping into one of the chairs facing Chance's desk.

"Your hair and that face." Chance leaned back in his chair and propped his feet, ankles crossed, on the end of his desk.

Ted gave him a baffled look. "What face?"

"The one under your messed-up hair," Chance told him, pointing the hand holding his coffee cup. "It looks like you've been shoving your hands through it and trying to pull it out."

"Hell." Ted grunted and ran his palm over the crown of his head. "Better?"

Chance shrugged. "Now tell me what's wrong."

"I've heard some bad news," Ted said gloomily.

"The lab test results on our latest research weren't what we hoped they'd be?" His mind was already thinking of options if this was the problem. They could try a new theory he'd been working on.... He was beginning to wonder whether the lower percentage of viable pregnancies from the current in vitro procedure might be solved with adding more specific vitamins and minerals to optimize the mother's health six months prior to conception. The lab tests so far seemed to indicate their current limited specific regimen was working.

"No, they're fine. Pretty much right on target."

Chance stared at him. "All...right," he said slowly, giving Ted time to spill his knowledge without prodding.

"Sara Beth told me a secret audit was conducted at the institute. The results show significant financial problems."

"Damn." Chance looked stunned. "Is she sure about this?"

Ted nodded. "Lisa told her about it."

"Pretty reliable source," Chance said. Lisa Armstrong wasn't only a member of the institute's founding family, she also was the head administrator for the medical facility. If Lisa had told Ted's wife, then the story was probably true. "Did Lisa say anything else?"

"Evidently the problems are severe enough that the institute's financial survival is at stake."

Chance swore again with feeling. "How could this have happened? I heard the Founder's Ball was a success at raising funds and donations have increased. What the hell's going on?"

"It doesn't seem to add up, does it?" Ted agreed, eyes narrowing in thought.

"No, it doesn't," Chance agreed. He thrust his fingers through his hair, raking it back off his forehead. "This comes at a critical point in our research," he said grimly. "I don't want to think about what would happen if we had to start all over at another lab."

"I know," Ted agreed morosely. "It could set us back months, if not years."

"I can't believe how many scandals the institute has been hit with over the past months," Chance commented. "It's amazing it hasn't sunk beneath the weight of bad news."

Ted nodded as he took a swig of coffee, his mouth grim. "I have to believe it will survive—after all, look how many storms it's weathered over the years."

"I hope you're right." Chance dropped his feet to

the floor and stood. "In the meantime, I suggest we go down to the lab and take a look at those test results."

For the rest of the day, Chance immersed himself in the work that both challenged and frustrated both he and Ted. The meticulous lab work from a large group of volunteer patients was time consuming and sometimes tedious but necessary if they were to prove their theory. The opportunity to increase a couple's chance to conceive and have a healthy baby was worth it to both men.

Later that evening, he headed for Jennifer's apartment, stopping on the way to pick up a family movie on DVD and a pizza. It didn't escape his notice that lately, when confronted with problems at work, he instinctively turned to Jennifer.

She opened the door with a smile and he bent to catch her in a quick, hard hug. She slipped her arms around his waist and held him tight for a moment before he released her.

"Is everything okay?" she asked, her warm blue gaze scanning his face.

"Just some problems at work," he told her. "And now that I'm here, I feel better already."

"Good." She caught his hand and drew him into the apartment. "Annie," she called as she closed the door behind him. "Chance is here."

"Goodie." The little girl bounced into the room, eyes lighting when she saw the box he carried. "Pizza!"

Chance grinned, handing her the DVD case to carry. She danced around him, waving the movie over her head, as he carried the pizza to the kitchen table. Jennifer took down plates, glasses and silverware.

"Can we eat in the living room while we watch the movie, Mommy? Please?" Annie pleaded, showing her mother the movie case.

"All right, just this once."

They transferred pizza slices to plates, filled glasses with ice water and settled on the sofa as the movie credits began to roll. When the plates and glasses were empty, Annie stretched out on the floor, chin on her hand, to watch the movie.

Chance helped Jennifer carry the dinner things into the kitchen and load them into the dishwasher. Just as they finished, the telephone rang.

"Go back and watch the movie," Jennifer told him. "I'll join you as soon as I take this call."

He brushed a kiss against her mouth and walked into the living room, dropping onto the sofa just as Jennifer picked up the phone.

Glancing sideways, he saw her slim body stiffen and her mouth tighten just before she turned her back, murmuring into the phone.

Curiosity piqued, he only half listened to the movie dialogue and still Jennifer's conversation in the kitchen was inaudible. But her body language was loud and clear.

"Everything okay?" he asked when she joined him on the sofa.

"Fine." She gave him a brief smile before she tucked her feet beneath her on the cushion.

Chance slipped his arm around her shoulder and eased her back until her shoulders were against his chest, her hair brushing his throat.

He'd wait until Annie was asleep, he decided. But regardless of what Jennifer had said, he knew by her pale face and the worry in her eyes that everything in her world was not "fine."

Two hours later, Annie was tucked into bed. Chance hit the mute button on the TV control and turned on the sofa to face Jennifer.

"Tell me about the call you got earlier," he suggested.

Her gaze flew to meet his, her eyes widening.

"You could tell me it was no one, and nothing," he went on. "But I saw your face after you hung up and I know the call upset you. So, tell me," he urged. He nudged her backward and lifted her feet into his lap, big hands kneading her stocking-covered feet.

"Umm, that's positively decadent," she murmured, half closing her eyes on a deep sigh.

"Yeah, yeah," he told her. "No changing the subject. Tell me what it was about that phone call the bothered you."

She opened her eyes and looked at him, her face somber. "It was my ex-husband."

Chance's hands stilled, then returned to kneading her instep. "I didn't know you two were still in touch."

"We aren't—at least, we haven't been since the divorce," she stated. "But this is the third time I've heard from him in the past month."

"What does he want?" Chance asked, frowning.

"You won't believe it," she warned him. "It's just too ridiculous."

"Tell me," he commanded gently.

"Patrick saw the photo of us dancing at the Founder's Ball. He's recently finished med school and applied for a position at the institute, and he wants me to ask you to hire him."

Her words were blunt, straightforward, but without inflection.

"I have the distinct impression that you're not telling me the whole truth," Chance said gently, circling his thumb over her arch, just below her toes.

"You're amazingly good at that," she sighed, stretching with a moan.

His thumbs stilled, poised motionless over her foot. "You're avoiding the subject again."

"All right, all right, I'll tell you. Please don't stop rubbing my foot."

"Fine." He stroked her arch and she nearly purred. "Tell me the rest of it."

"He threatened me with Annie."

"What?" Chance stopped rubbing her foot and leaned over her to grab her shoulders.

"Hey." Jennifer's eyes rounded.

"Sorry," he muttered, easing back a foot and patting her shoulder awkwardly before gently cupping her chin in one hand. "Tell me what he said about Annie."

"He threatened to take me back to court and sue to get visitation."

"I thought he voluntarily gave up any rights as her father when you two were divorced?"

"He agreed to leave us alone if I agreed to never ask him for child support," Jennifer corrected. "I was pregnant when he filed for divorce and he listed our marriage as 'without children.'"

"What a jerk," Chance ground out. "Why did you marry the guy? What could have attracted a smart, savvy woman like you to him?"

"You think I'm smart and savvy?" Her smile was brilliant, her eyes meltingly warm.

"Of course I do. And don't change the subject," he told her for the third time.

"I was very young and he was very charming. Not a good excuse, obviously, but the truth is that I was naive and fell for the wonderful exterior. My only defense is that I left when I discovered that Patrick's interior wasn't so great." She paused. "But the marriage wasn't a total loss—because it gave me Annie."

"It sounds to me like that's your ex's one redeeming feature," he told her. "I thought he'd signed away his parental rights but evidently he never did?"

"No, he didn't." Jennifer's eyes darkened. "Frankly, it never occurred to me that he'd want to exercise his rights as her father. He's never even seen her—never wanted to. And he doesn't really want anything to do with her now. He's just using Annie as a means to force me to cooperate." Her gaze turned fierce. "Let's make something clear, Chance. I am *not* asking you to help Patrick get a job at the institute. I don't know what I'll do about him threatening Annie but I'm hoping he'll drop the whole thing when he realizes it won't get him anywhere."

"Honey, it never occurred to me that you'd cooperate with him," Chance declared. "And neither will I." He pulled her into his arms, her slim body lying trustingly against his. "I don't want you to worry about Annie. We'll figure out a way to stop him. If we need to, I'll call my family's legal representatives. They've never lost a case for the family yet."

Jennifer pressed closer. Chance slid his fingers into the silk of her hair and tugged gently, tipping her face up to his.

"No one's going to threaten you and Annie." His tone was fierce but the kisses he brushed against the corner of her mouth were gentle, soothing. He felt her sigh and stir against him, her lips seeking his.

A half hour later, they were both aroused, breathing unevenly and too fast, when Chance sighed and pulled Jennifer up from the sofa.

"Unless you're going to take me to bed, I'd better go home. I only have so much control and I've about used up my quota for the night."

"Chance, I'm not sure…" she began.

He stopped her by laying his finger against her lips, damp from the press of his.

"I know. You're not ready." He tucked her against his side and walked to the door. The kiss he gave her before pulling open the door sizzled with heat and frustrated longing. "Lock the door after me," he told her as he stepped outside.

"Good night," she murmured.

"I'll see you tomorrow," he told her. He waited until he heard the locks click shut then moved down the hallway.

Before he reached his car, he'd placed a call on his cell phone to the investigative agency his father used. Assured they would locate Jennifer's ex-husband by tomorrow morning, Chance drove home, his mind churning with how to remove the man from her life for good.

By the time he reached his town house, he knew exactly how he wanted to proceed.

"Dr. Demetrios, your three-o'clock appointment is here."

"Send him in." Chance flicked off the intercom and leaned back in his chair. Except for a thin file and a pen directly in front of him, the polished expanse of mahogany desktop was bare, creating a wide barrier between him and the group of four leather armchairs facing the desk.

The door opened and a man entered.

Chance stood slowly, assessing Jennifer's ex-husband. He was medium height with a compact body and he wore an expensive gray suit with a conservative blue silk tie. His features were boyish and he had an affable smile that Chance shrewdly suspected would charm women.

Chance disliked him on sight.

"Patrick Evans?"

"Yes." Patrick reached the desk and the two men exchanged a quick handshake. "It's a pleasure to meet you, Dr. Demetrios. I've followed your work here with great interest over the past several months."

"Thanks. Sit down." Chance waved him to a chair and resumed his seat behind the desk. He tapped the file in front of him with his forefinger. "Your application states you've recently completed your residency at Chicago General. What made you decide to apply to the Armstrong Fertility Institute for your first position?"

"Your research," Patrick said promptly. "I'm very interested in emerging methods of in vitro procedures and the efficacy of the process. The Armstrong Institute is on the cutting edge of research in the field. I want to be part of the team."

He punctuated his comments with a sincere smile.

"I see," Chance said evenly. "I understand you were once married to Jennifer Lebeaux."

"Yes, I was." Patrick's expression turned wryly regretful. "We were too young and the marriage didn't last, unfortunately."

"Hmm," Chance said noncommittally. He wasn't surprised that Patrick had a ready, glib response since he could have anticipated Jennifer would tell Chance about their marriage. Still, his fingers half curled into fists before he purposely straightened them. "And you have a daughter?"

"Yes, her name is Annie." Patrick shifted in his chair and his features reflected a faint sadness. "Circumstances have kept me from seeing her as much as I'd like, but now that my residency is finished, I hope to change that."

Chance had heard enough and seen enough phony emotion from Patrick. His original analysis of Jennifer's ex-husband hadn't changed with a face-to-face meeting. The man was an ass who didn't give a damn about Annie.

"I suggest you rethink your relationship to Annie." Chance's neutral tone shifted, an undercurrent of menace running through his words.

Patrick blinked. "I beg your pardon?" he said warily.

"I've had my attorney draw up two documents. You will sign them, relinquish all parental rights to Annie and agree to her adoption by a man who is capable of being a real father to her."

Patrick shoved back his chair and stood, anger painting flags of red across his cheekbones. "What makes you think you can order me to sign anything?"

Chance stood, leaning forward to plant his fists on the glossy desktop. He made no attempt to conceal the contempt he felt. "I have the power to keep you from being hired in damn near every research facility on the eastern seaboard, maybe even in the entire U.S."

"You can't do that," Patrick protested. But his color faded and his eyes shifted to the file, then back to Chance.

"Try me." Chance's voice deepened, turned more lethal. "And if you ever threaten Jennifer or Annie again, I won't waste time calling your boss or my attorney. I'll come looking for you myself."

"Just because you're a Demetrios doesn't mean you can get away with forcing me to sign away my rights to my child," he blustered. Color ebbed and flowed in the younger man's face, mottling and changing the boyish good looks with sulky dislike.

"I don't need my family's money or good name to take care of you. But I'll use whatever I have to," Chance said grimly. He opened the file and took out two legal documents, sliding them across the desktop, the pen on top. "We both know you couldn't care less about Annie or Jennifer. Sign the consent papers."

Patrick glared at him for a moment in one last gesture of obstinacy and stubbornness before he snatched up the pen. The writing was fast, slight shaky, and then he shoved the documents back across the desk to Chance.

Chance flipped the pages, making sure they were signed properly, then slid them into the file.

"I have your word you won't blacklist me with your friends at other research facilities?" Patrick demanded with belligerence.

"You do."

The other man turned on his heel and strode to the door, yanking it open.

"If any of this conversation leaks, I'll know who spread the rumors. And if I find out you've talked," Chance said with lethal intent, "all bets are off. I'd take a great deal of pleasure in making sure you never practice medicine."

Patrick's face whitened. Without a word, he left the room, closing the door quietly behind him.

Muscles tight with the effort it had taken to keep from throwing Patrick physically out of his office, Chance forcibly unclenched his fists and rolled his shoulders. Adrenaline still surged through his veins and he strode to the window to look down on the parking lot below. He waited until Patrick exited the building, climbed into a sedan and drove with a rush of speed out of the lot.

"So much for Patrick Evans," Chance muttered aloud. He knew a deep sense of satisfaction that the man no longer had any claim on Jennifer or Annie. The documents he'd signed only legally established what Chance was convinced had always been true—Evans had never really loved Jennifer or their daughter.

What a fool the man is, he thought. If he'd ever been lucky enough to have a wife and child like Jennifer and Annie, he never would have let them go.

And I won't now, he thought with sudden clarity and fierce determination. He wanted Jennifer and her little girl in his life permanently, here in his home, sharing his life. He wanted the legal right to protect them both—and that meant marriage and Annie's adoption.

He didn't know how long he'd been thinking of Jennifer as his but he knew he wasn't going to wait to make her his.

He just hoped she felt the same.

He caught up the file and headed for the door, intent on driving directly to Jennifer's apartment to talk to her. He just stepped over the threshold when his secretary hurried toward him.

"Chance, there's an emergency with Mrs. Mac-

Quillen. Her husband called 911 and the ambulance is taking her directly to the hospital."

"I'm on my way." Chance strode off down the hallway, punching in numbers on his cell phone as he went. Much as he wanted to see Jennifer, his patient came first. Ralph MacQuillen answered on the third ring, his voice distracted. "Ralph, this is Dr. Demetrios."

Chance calmed the anxious husband and told him they'd meet at the hospital. Moments later, he drove out of the parking lot, knowing it may be hours before he could talk to Jennifer, his mind switching to Mrs. MacQuillen's pregnancy.

Earlier that same day, Jennifer tried to reach Chance at his office but was told he was out. Dashing out the door to catch the bus to work, she wondered where he was and hoped he'd come by the apartment later that evening. She didn't have a class and over the past three weeks, she'd come to count on seeing Chance on her free nights.

I wonder if that means this is a relationship, she wondered.

Later that evening, the hour grew late and Chance didn't appear. Disappointed, Jennifer bathed Annie before reading two chapters from an Eloise book and turning off the light.

Alone in the darkened living room, she clicked through channels on the TV, finding nothing that caught her interest.

She missed Chance, she realized. Resolutely, she located a mystery series and tried to concentrate on the story.

Just after 10:00 p.m., someone rapped on her door. After checking her visitor through the door's peephole, Jennifer pulled open the door.

"Hi." She held the door wide and Chance entered.

He pushed the door shut and dragged her close, wrapping her tightly against his body while his mouth covered hers.

"Hi," he rasped when he finally lifted his head. "Did you miss me?"

She laughed. "It hasn't even been twenty-four hours but yes, I missed you. I thought you would be here earlier."

"I've been busy," he told her. "Making sure your ex-husband can never threaten you or Annie again."

Her eyes widened. "Chance, what have you done?" Worry veed her brows as she frowned. "You didn't buy him off, did you? I didn't want you to give in to his blackmail. If you helped him get a job at the institute, you'd never be able to trust him."

"I didn't do what he wanted," Chance assured her.

He reached into the inner pocket of his leather jacket, removed a folded sheaf of papers and handed them to her. "These are for you."

Confused, Jennifer took the papers, unfolding them as Chance shrugged out of his jacket and tossed it over the seat of the rocking chair.

She read the legal documents twice, hardly daring to believe what she thought the wording meant. The documents were signed by Patrick and stated that he abandoned his legal parental rights to Annie and specifically agreed to an adoption.

"I don't know what to say," she said, stunned. "How did you convince Patrick to do this?"

"It was simple," he told her. "I threatened to tell certain influential people at the best research facilities in his field that he wasn't a good candidate." Chance shrugged. "I'm not without influence in the arena and he knows it. So he agreed to give up Annie." His face tightened, a muscle flexing along his jawline. "In return, I said I'd refrain from discussing his lack of character with potential employers. And I didn't think he and the institute were a good fit."

"Oh, Chance…" Jennifer's mouth trembled and tears welled, threatening to spill down her cheeks.

"Don't cry, honey." He pulled her into his arms

and she burrowed closer, pressing her tear-damp face against his throat. He cupped the back of her head in one big hand. "I'm not sure you're ready to hear this, but I need to say it. I want to marry you and adopt Annie."

She tipped her head back, her gaze searching his. His dark brown eyes were fierce with conviction.

"Say yes, Jennifer. I'm in love for the first—and last—time in my life. Living without you isn't an option." His arms tightened, pressing her closer.

"I didn't know—you didn't tell me you loved me," she whispered.

A wry half smile curved his mouth. "I didn't think you were ready to hear it. Plus, I've never felt this way about a woman before, not the way I have you. I guess I thought it was obvious I was head over heels in love with you."

"Not to me," she murmured. "But maybe that's because I'm head over heels in love with you, too."

His fingers flexed in reaction, stroking her sensitized skin.

"I'm glad you said that," he muttered with a sigh of relief. "Because if you didn't, I had no plan for what to do next."

"What was your plan if I said yes?" she asked, smiling as she turned her head and kissed the warm, strong column of his throat, breathing in the faint trace of cologne and a scent that was his alone. Her heart raced, thudding in her chest.

"I was hoping you'd take me to bed." He tilted his head back to look down at her, arousal painting a slash of color over the arch of his cheekbones. "I haven't pressed you because I know you vowed Annie would never wake and find you in bed with someone—and I respect that decision. But we're going to be married, as soon as possible, I hope. And I don't want to leave you tonight."

"And after tonight?" she asked, holding on to the moment.

"I want us to elope—you and Annie and me. And I want you to move in with me. I have plenty of room at my house." He smoothed the pad of his thumb over her cheekbone. "Say yes, Jennifer. I don't want to spend any more nights without you."

"Yes." She smiled through misty tears. "Yes, I'll marry you."

He grinned, dark eyes lighting. "I feel like I've just won the lottery." He pressed a hard kiss against her mouth. "Annie's going to love living with Butch and he'll be crazy about having her there," he said when he lifted his head.

"We'll have trouble separating them at night," she agreed.

"I vote for not fighting that battle. Let's just move Butch's bed into her room," Chance said dryly.

"You know Annie so well." She laughed.

With decision, she stepped back, taking his hand in hers. "Come to bed with me, Chance," she murmured, relishing the words. "And stay until the morning. When Annie gets up, we can all have breakfast together and tell her the news."

His eyes darkened to black, fierce emotion filling them.

She led him into the bedroom, to her turned-down sheets and comfortable bed—the bed that she'd slept in alone since before Annie was born.

But no longer. Chance's broad shoulders and big body would crowd her bed just as his love filled her heart.

As he tugged her T-shirt over her head and bent to take her mouth with his, Jennifer was swamped with a rush of emotion. Chance made her feel all the things she never thought she'd be—happy, safe, cherished, challenged and loved.

Just before he stripped off their clothes and lowered her onto the bed, she vowed she would love and cherish him, as well. The future glowed with promise, bright and beckoning.

It seemed she'd finally found her Prince Charming.

* * * * *

Look for the next installment in the new
Special Edition continuity,
THE BABY CHASE
Attorney Hector Garza is stunned when his
former neighbor moves back to Boston.
He'd long harbored a crush on beautiful
Samantha Keating and is hoping her return
will mean a second chance. But then Samantha
reveals that she's pregnant—with triplets!
Will Hector be up to the challenge of instant
fatherhood with the woman who owns his heart?
Don't miss
AND BABIES MAKE FIVE
By Judy Duarte.
On sale May 2010,
wherever Silhouette Books are sold.

*Harlequin Intrigue top author Delores Fossen
presents a brand-new series of
breathtaking romantic suspense!*
TEXAS MATERNITY: HOSTAGES
*The first installment available May 2010:
THE BABY'S GUARDIAN*

Shaw cursed and hooked his arm around Sabrina.

Despite the urgency that the deadly gunfire created, he tried to be careful with her, and he took the brunt of the fall when he pulled her to the ground. His shoulder hit hard, but he held on tight to his gun so that it wouldn't be jarred from his hand.

Shaw didn't stop there. He crawled over Sabrina, sheltering her pregnant belly with his body, and he came up ready to return fire.

This was obviously a situation he'd wanted to avoid at all cost. He didn't want his baby in the middle of a fight with these armed fugitives, but when they fired that shot, they'd left him no choice. Now, the trick was to get Sabrina safely out of there.

"Get down," someone on the SWAT team yelled from the roof of the adjacent building.

Shaw did. He dropped lower, covering Sabrina as best he could.

There was another shot, but this one came from a rifleman on the SWAT team. Shaw didn't look up, but he heard the sound of glass being blown apart.

The shots continued, all coming from his men, which meant it might be time to try to get Sabrina to better cover. Shaw glanced at the front of the building.

So that Sabrina's pregnant belly wouldn't be smashed against the ground, Shaw eased off her and moved her to a sitting position so that her back was against the brick wall. They were close. Too close. And face-to-face.

He found himself staring right into those sea-green eyes.

How will Shaw get Sabrina out?
Follow the daring rescue and the heartbreaking
aftermath in THE BABY'S GUARDIAN
by Delores Fossen,
available May 2010 from Harlequin Intrigue.

Copyright © 2010 by Delores Fossen

is proud to introduce...

New York Times bestselling author

Brenda Jackson

with
SPONTANEOUS

Kim Cannon and Duan Jeffries have a great thing going.
Whenever they meet up, the passion between them
is hot, intense…spontaneous. And things really heat
up when Duan agrees to accompany her to her
mother's wedding. Too bad there's something
he's not telling her.…

Don't miss the fireworks!

*Available in May 2010
wherever Harlequin Blaze books are sold.*

red-hot reads

www.eHarlequin.com

HB79542

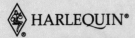

HARLEQUIN®

American ★ Romance®

LAURA MARIE ALTOM

The Baby Twins

Stephanie Olmstead has her hands full raising her twin baby girls on her own. When she runs into old friend Brady Flynn, she's shocked to find herself suddenly attracted to the handsome airline pilot! Will this flyboy be the perfect daddy— or will he crash and burn?

Babies
&
Bachelors
USA

"LOVE, HOME & HAPPINESS"

www.eHarlequin.com

HAR75309

HARLEQUIN
Ambassadors

Want to share your passion for reading Harlequin® Books?

Become a Harlequin Ambassador!

Harlequin Ambassadors are a group of passionate and well-connected readers who are willing to share their joy of reading Harlequin® books with family and friends.

You'll be sent all the tools you need to spark great conversation, including free books!

All we ask is that you share the romance with your friends and family!

You'll also be invited to have a say in new book ideas and exchange opinions with women just like you!

To see if you qualify* to be a Harlequin Ambassador, please visit www.HarlequinAmbassadors.com.

*Please note that not everyone who applies to be a Harlequin Ambassador will qualify. For more information please visit www.HarlequinAmbassadors.com.

Thank you for your participation.

BAPX9BPA

◆ HARLEQUIN®

INTRIGUE®

**BESTSELLING
HARLEQUIN INTRIGUE® AUTHOR**

DELORES FOSSEN

**PRESENTS AN ALL-NEW
THRILLING TRILOGY**

TEXAS MATERNITY: HOSTAGES

When masked gunmen take over the maternity ward at a San Antonio hospital, local cops, FBI and the scared mothers can't figure out any possible motive. Before long, secrets are revealed, and a city that has been on edge since the siege began learns the truth behind the negotiations and must deal with the fallout.

LOOK FOR

THE BABY'S GUARDIAN, *May*
DEVASTATING DADDY, *June*
THE MOMMY MYSTERY, *July*

www.eHarlequin.com   HI69472

Love Inspired

Former bad boy Sloan Hawkins is back in
Redemption, Oklahoma, to help keep his aunt's
cherished garden thriving and to reconnect with the
girl he left behind, Annie Markham. But when he
discovers his secret child—and that single mother
Annie never stopped loving him—he's determined
that a wedding will take place in the garden
nurtured by faith and love.

REDEMPTION RIVER

Where healing flows...

Look for

The Wedding Garden
by Linda Goodnight

Available May 2010
wherever you buy books.

www.SteepleHill.com

Steeple
Hill®
LI87595

Bestselling Harlequin Presents® author

Lynne Graham

introduces

VIRGIN ON HER WEDDING NIGHT

Valente Lorenzatto never forgave Caroline Hales's
abandonment of him at the altar. But now he's
made millions and claimed his aristocratic Venetian
birthright—and he's poised to get his revenge.
He'll ruin Caroline's family by buying out their
company and throwing them out of their mansion...
unless she agrees to give him the wedding night
she denied him five years ago....

**Available May 2010
from Harlequin Presents!**

www.eHarlequin.com

HP12915

REQUEST YOUR FREE BOOKS!
2 FREE NOVELS PLUS 2 FREE GIFTS!

SPECIAL EDITION
Life, Love and Family!

YES! Please send me 2 FREE Silhouette® Special Edition® novels and my 2 FREE gifts (gifts are worth about $10). After receiving them, if I don't wish to receive any more books, I can return the shipping statement marked "cancel." If I don't cancel, I will receive 6 brand-new novels every month and be billed just $4.24 per book in the U.S. or $4.99 per book in Canada. That's a saving of 15% off the cover price! It's quite a bargain! Shipping and handling is just 50¢ per book.* I understand that accepting the 2 free books and gifts places me under no obligation to buy anything. I can always return a shipment and cancel at any time. Even if I never buy another book from Silhouette, the two free books and gifts are mine to keep forever.

235/335 SDN E5RG

Name _____ (PLEASE PRINT)

Address _____ Apt. #

City _____ State/Prov. _____ Zip/Postal Code _____

Signature (if under 18, a parent or guardian must sign)

Mail to the **Silhouette Reader Service:**
IN U.S.A.: P.O. Box 1867, Buffalo, NY 14240-1867
IN CANADA: P.O. Box 609, Fort Erie, Ontario L2A 5X3

Not valid for current subscribers to Silhouette Special Edition books.

Want to try two free books from another line?
Call 1-800-873-8635 or visit www.morefreebooks.com.

* Terms and prices subject to change without notice. Prices do not include applicable taxes. N.Y. residents add applicable sales tax. Canadian residents will be charged applicable provincial taxes and GST. Offer not valid in Quebec. This offer is limited to one order per household. All orders subject to approval. Credit or debit balances in a customer's account(s) may be offset by any other outstanding balance owed by or to the customer. Please allow 4 to 6 weeks for delivery. Offer available while quantities last.

Your Privacy: Silhouette is committed to protecting your privacy. Our Privacy Policy is available online at www.eHarlequin.com or upon request from the Reader Service. From time to time we make our lists of customers available to reputable third parties who may have a product or service of interest to you. If you would prefer we not share your name and address, please check here. ☐

Help us get it right—We strive for accurate, respectful and relevant communications. To clarify or modify your communication preferences, visit us at www.ReaderService.com/consumerschoice.

SSE10R